ONE SAUSALITO SUMMER

A NOVEL

Colleen Rae

ONE SAUSALITO SUMMER
© Colleen Rae, 2016

Cover art by Alan Angeloff

Book design by Jo-Anne Rosen

ISBN: 978-1-941066-11-9

Wordrunner Press
Petaluma, California

Acknowledgments

*T*his novel is based on a true story. Some incidents were added that did not happen, therefore it is a work of fiction. Certain musicians written about in this novel later went on to join or create several West Coast Rock Bands in the 1960s. For obvious reasons I changed their identities. All of the bands mentioned did exist during that time period, except for The Desperados and the Sunny Day Band.

I want to thank Rosie Sorenson for her very helpful suggestions and reading of the novel. She is a fine writer in her own right, author of *They Had Me at Meow*, and *Tails of Love from Homeless Cats*, who took time to read my work as a friend.

Also thanks to Kathryn Jennings, a long-time friend, for reading the novel and making suggestions and correcting errors.

Jo-Anne Rosen of Wordrunner Press has always contributed a great deal in designing and formatting my books and again she made the process go smoothly for me.

The unique cover art was created by artist Alan Angeloff, a dear friend who also helped tirelessly with proof editing.

Alberta is a traditional folk song. All other words to songs were created by the author.

The five lines read at Jesse's funeral were written by William Shakespeare.

Last but not least, I owe a huge debt of gratitude and thanks to my good friend and mentor Guy Biederman, creator of *Bust Out Stories* and author of *House Samurai*, a book of poetry, for teaching me the fundamentals of novel writing and for his excellent copy edit.

For the wonderful man

in my life, Larry.

Life on the

Charles Van Damme Boat

1

"Alberta let your hair hang low…" Cass's soprano voice with a trembling vibrato floated across the coffee house like a magic carpet. People said she sounded a little like Joan Baez. The beat-up guitar had a rich quality and she played it simply, stroking chords to a traditional folk song.

On the next verse she forgot the words and hummed in that high pitch, perfect tone.

Then she remembered… "I'll bring you more gold than your apron can hold; Alberta let your hair hang low." Her voice rang out on the minor notes in a mournful tone.

She'd smoked a joint before going onstage.

Swirls of marijuana and cigarette smoke intertwined and drifted around the ceiling. She smelled the sharp aroma of Turkish coffee beans being ground in the back. Her long brunette hair hung around her face like a cloak, occasionally touching the guitar. Leaning into the song, she came through with emotion, not seeming to care if she forgot the words. Her dark eyes closed in a rapt moment. The muumuu she wore draped around her slim body.

She had been singing on a dry-docked ferry boat, The Charles Van Damme in Sausalito, California for three days. A coffee house, referred to by the 'in' crowd as, The Ark, had been set up on the upper deck. Coffee and tea were served, and even though they didn't have a liquor license, bottles of booze sat on every table, along with dishes and mirrors full of a white substance that Cass didn't have a clue to what it was. Since she was ignorant, she left it alone.

Thinking back to the first time she sang on the boat she tried smoking a joint and didn't get high, coughing in great gasps. She looked around at everyone else who seemed to be having a terrific time. One of the musicians saw her and came over.

"You didn't get high?" he asked.

She shook her head.

"Open your mouth." He took a hit off a joint and blew the smoke down her throat, then closed her lips with his fingers.

"Inhale," he ordered.

It took a few times and finally she felt the smooth high envelop her.

"Kind of like kissing," he said as he buzzed her lips in a soft peck.

After that, she was able to get high when she took a hit.

"What's your name," he asked.

"Cass."

"Mine's Jesse."

"Thanks, Jesse."

"You bet darlin'."

Jesse owned a wild, curly afro streaked with blond, his face wore a perpetual look of wonderment. Around his neck he wore three or four strands of Turquoise, and Turquoise bracelets on his wrists. He was a few inches taller than Cass and played a bitchin' 12 string guitar.

Cass's attention was drawn to the stage. Local musicians the likes of Dino Valenti, David Crosby, and John Cipollina dropped by to sing for free and often would jam all night. Cass had no idea who they were. Unknowns were also welcome, so Cass took the stage early in the evening. She didn't know that the professional musicians played later. However, hearing the great jamming, she was hesitant to get up again to perform.

Jesse encouraged her. "Go ahead and sing. We all like to hear your lovely voice." She smoked some grass, took the stage, forgot the words but stumbled through two songs. Then another amateur got up and sang, *Lay Lady Lay*, a Dylan song. This went on for several hours until the amateurs were finished. Then the real music started.

⤳

Cass came to the Bay Area from Southern California with her friend Lia, a college student at UCLA. They drove up in Lia's little red MG with no top. Lia was tiny, about five foot and she fit in the car easily. Cass was five foot seven, and had to cram her legs beneath the dash. The passenger door was wired shut so Cass climbed over it.

Lia's boyfriend, Howard Bateman managed the old ferry boat, The Charles Van Damme, for the summer.

Arriving in the early evening, the girls found Gate Six at Waldo Point easily. Howard happened to be on deck and saw them drive up as Cass and Lia walked up the gangplank. He greeted Lia with open arms. Howard was a tall, handsome, man who had been outdoors much of his life. His tanned, weathered face only added to his rugged good looks. He was married and had a couple of kids in San Francisco, but his wife Faye was pretty open-minded. Or so it seemed, then.

"This is my friend, Cass," Lia said to Howard.

He looked straight at her with a lopsided smile. "Hi, I'm Howard. Come on in the wheel house and I'll light a joint."

They followed him into the little aft cabin. There was a large bed that took up most of the space. A bench and a mahogany ship's wheel took up the rest.

Howard rolled a joint with skill and lit it with a Zippo. When it was passed to Cass she declined.

"Never smoked before?" He asked.

Cass shook her head.

"Well, you'd better learn how."

"Later," she said. "Where can I find a bathroom?"

"Here on the boat, we call it a head. Go out on deck and turn right. You'll find it."

She left them, sensing that they wanted to be alone and she wasn't ready for her first joint.

The boat listed slightly so it made walking on deck unsteady. She found the head, a stool and basin, and a tiny shower.

Leaving the head, she took a walk down below. There were primitive rooms with bunk beds on each level. Plenty of room to sleep. Later she would find plenty of dope of all kinds, plenty of music, and booze, and plenty of young, good looking men and women roaming the boat for a companion or a high.

Cass found a room to crash in that seemed a little cleaner than the rest, but there was no lock on the door. The first night as she slept she felt skin touch her skin and woke up immediately. A little disoriented at new sleeping quarters, it suddenly registered that someone was in her bed.

When she felt a hand on her breast, she sat up and screamed. "Get out!"

"Okay, okay, hang loose, babe." A young man climbed out of bed and left the room. After that, she pulled an old trunk against the door.

After her heart settled down to a normal rate she got back in bed and mused on the unconventionality of this boat. Anything seemed to be okay. She wasn't going for that kind of behavior. At least she wanted to know the person before she shared her bed with him.

After the first night she sang, Cass walked down Bridgeway to The Kettle Deli for some food. When she got back to the boat the music was in full swing.

She stayed in the coffee house into the wee hours listening to the musicians jam. The guy that had showed her how to inhale, Jesse, played a 12-string, knew some wonderful songs, some of which he had written. His trusty black Lab, Kayak came and lay beside his chair all night. Lia spent much of her time in the wheelhouse with Howard.

When the dishes of white stuff were handed around she passed on it not knowing what it was. Some of the substance was snorted with a dollar bill. She saw one guy mix some substance with water and draw it up into a needle and then shoot it into his arm. That made Cass shiver. She had never seen that before, but she had read about it. Later when Jesse was beside her and the dish of white stuff was passed, he snorted some with a dollar bill, then he handed it to her and she decided to do the same.

A strange cross between pain and pleasure shot up her nose. Then a rush that made her feel hot and flushed. She felt it between her legs in a sexual throb. Leaning back, she enjoyed the heady experience. The colors of the coffee house raced across her vision and she became excited by the reds and blues of the décor. Her nose seemed to become super-sensitive; she thought she could smell the sweat on Jesse's skin. The intensity of the music was heightened and she felt like she was floating across the room on the melody. Her vision became glazed, and wetness seeped into her eyes.

"This is Cocaine," he told her. "Don't do this very often. It's addictive."

After that, she could sing for hours and her voice had a lovely quality to it. Or so she thought.

When she grew tired and her muscles began to ache

she crept off to her room and climbed into the lower bunk bed. However she couldn't go to sleep. Who knew — certainly she didn't being a novice — that Cocaine kept you awake?

A few hours later she made her way back on deck to the coffee house. All the musicians were gone or passed out on the couches. Jesse was not there. There was no one else awake. People were sprawled on deck chairs and lounges. The acrid odor of cigarettes and marijuana was heavy in the air.

She sneaked up to the shower beside the wheel-house and had a quick sudsing, then went back to bed to see if she could relax. Finally sleep came.

2

The Charles Van Damme ferry boat was towed to Gate Six in Sausalito at Waldo Point in 1960 and first became a restaurant, Juanita's Galley, and then a coffee house called The Ark. Lia's boyfriend Howard, obtained permission from the owner to start a coffee house on the boat during the summer of 1963. Sometimes the entire boat was referred to as The Ark.

When Lia suggested Cass come with her to Sausalito and she could sing on the boat, it sounded like an adventurous idea. She was restless since she'd quit her job as a second string reporter with the Los Angeles Times.

Lia met Howard at a rock concert in Los Angeles earlier that year. They bonded in the crowd and spent a week together at her place in Westwood. Then Howard returned to the Bay Area and they stayed in touch.

Life on the Van Damme boat revolved around nights; everyone came to drink, snort dope, sing, play and listen to music. Cass soon got into the rhythm of it and got high every night. She would sleep until noon and then wander off the boat for breakfast to some eating place within walking distance. The Kettle Deli was nearby and she usually walked there. There were other people staying on the boat and often she was invited to join them. Sometimes she did and sometimes she ate alone.

She was eating an egg salad sandwich when Jesse sat down beside her.

"How's Sleeping Beauty?" he asked.

"Tired. I'm not used to this staying up all night and sleeping half of the day."

"It grows on you. Pretty soon you won't be able to go to sleep before 4 a.m."

"I have trouble getting to sleep."

"I got some pills that will put you to sleep. Remind me to give you some tonight."

The waitress came over and Jesse ordered a ham sandwich.

"What are they?" Cass asked.

"Sleeping pills for Sleeping Beauty." He smiled and stroked her back.

Cass felt a little uncomfortable at his easy camaraderie. She wasn't going to take pills that she didn't know about.

"I can come early and teach you a new song?" He offered.

Cass did want to learn some new tunes. "Will you teach me one of your songs?"

He smiled, "Sure."

"I'll teach you one that hasn't been published yet."

The waitress brought his order and he dug into his food. He pulled a flask from his jacket and took a long swallow.

"Want a swig?"

She shook her head. "No thanks. I'll wait for tonight."

Jesse scarfed up his sandwich and stood up, leaving a ten on the table.

"This should cover yours, too."

"You don't have to do that," she said.

"I know, I want to. I got to go see a man about some dope. See you tonight. Meet me on deck and we'll find a corner to practice."

She nodded and smiled, but she wasn't so sure she wanted to get that friendly with him. Then he was gone.

On her walk back to the boat, she started thinking about Jesse. He was good looking and he treated her well, and he was an excellent musician and had a low sexy voice, but she wasn't sure where this was going. She knew that sleeping with a guy these days meant nothing. Didn't mean they were a couple, just a casual thing. So did she want to do this casual thing? She'd had one relationship since she'd divorced Jack, her husband of five years, but that was over now. She was still getting her training wheels in shape.

Back on The Ark, Lia and Howard were on deck.

"Where you been?" Lia asked.

"Down at the Deli."

"Are you getting to know people here?"

Cass nodded. "Yeah, I met Jesse. He comes every night and jams with the rest of them."

"Jesse is a great guy," Howard said.

"He showed me how to inhale weed." Cass admitted.

Howard and Lia laughed.

"I'm glad your education is continuing. Anything else you've learned?"Lia asked.

Cass smiled smugly. "Yup. Learned to snort Cocaine."

That made Lia and Howard hoot with laughter. "Bitchin', you are getting educated," Howard said.

"I knew it was a good idea to bring you along. You were entirely too sheltered down there in L.A.," Lia said.

"What'd you do in L.A.," asked Howard.

"I just came off a divorce and I'm learning to be a single girl again."

"Got a job?" Howard asked.

"No, I just quit one, newspaper reporter. I don't want one yet. Luckily I got a nice settlement from my ex. I sing now and then at coffee houses around the beach area. The Insomniac Coffee House in Hermosa Beach is where I usually sing."

Howard put his arm around Lia. "How do you two know each other?"

"My ex-boyfriend worked with her ex-husband," Lia said. "We got to know each other through them."

"I hope you're enjoying yourself," Howard said. "There are lots of musicians here at night. You could pick up some new songs."

"Jesse said he'd teach me a new one tonight," Cass said.

"Watch out for Jesse. He's a ladies' man. He'll charm you into bed then leave you tomorrow morning." Howard laughed.

"Yes, I am aware of that. But thanks for the warning," Cass said.

"Let's go out and get some food, girl," Howard said to Lia.

They stood up, and walked down the gangplank arm in arm.

Cass watched them saunter down the pier to Bridgeway. She envied Lia in that she had a man who obviously cared for her. But Lia living in L.A. and Howard up here in the Bay Area did not bode well for a permanent relationship, besides his wife and two children. Cass had been in a permanent relationship for five years and it had been disappointing. She didn't want or need another one right away. Maybe some casual sex was just what she needed. Maybe if Jesse hit on her again, she'd take him up on it.

ᶜ

Cass was sitting on the deck watching and feeding the sea gulls small chunks of bread. The sun was beginning to set behind Mount Tamalpais casting orange and pink clouds across the San Francisco skyline.

She saw Jesse in the distance walking down the pier. He must have come from a boat. He was carrying his guitar case and his dog, Kayak walked just a step behind.

When he climbed on deck he saw Cass and waved. As he moved toward her she was again struck by his good looks. He had a boyish innocence that belied the experienced man he obviously was.

"Hi, girl." He sat down beside her and brought out a joint from his pocket. He lit it and passed it to her. Cass took a hit and passed it back.

"I see you got the hang of it now. I'm kind of sorry I

don't have to blow smoke in your mouth. Such a pretty mouth, too." His brown eyes twinkled.

Cass blushed. She wished she could kick herself for looking so pleased.

Jesse leaned down and kissed her lips. "Nice," he murmured.

Cass felt butterflies in her stomach but at the end of the kiss pushed him away.

"Hey, I'm going to learn a new song."

Jesse pulled back, opened his guitar case and took out his 12-string. "Okay, girl. Get your axe out and we'll tune up."

Cass picked up her guitar and they began tuning. She was slow so Jesse tuned her folk guitar to his 12-string.

Cass began learning one of his songs and they worked on it for an hour, going over each line twice so Cass could get it. Soon Jesse was taking off on his own and Cass was left behind in the swirl of guitar melodies. She put down her guitar and harmonized with Jesse.

At nine, the music started on The Ark. A young guy was first up to sing. He had a Woody Guthrie-type voice and sang songs about the dustbowl of yesteryear. Woody was definitely his influence.

Cass was humming the song Jesse taught her.

"Are you going to sing it? I'll play guitar if you want to," Jesse offered.

"I don't think so; I don't know it that well."

"I'll sing it with you, how's that?" Jesse was tuning one of his strings.

Cass decided to risk it. "Okay."

She and Jesse went onstage and he took a stool and she stood at the mike. After he played an intro rift, he nodded and they started singing.

"Better leave the stuff alone, makes your blood begin to moan..." Cass's lilting soprano floated above the audience like a wind chime. She thought they sounded good together.

After the song was finished, Jesse left the stage and Cass sang one of her regular songs; *Wish I Was a Single Girl Again*. She saw Jesse wave, put his guitar back in the case and leave The Ark. He moved his lips to say... "I'll be back." He and Kayak left.

After Cass had sung four songs she left the stage and sat down at a table.

"Nice voice," a dude said, sitting at the table.

"Thanks."

"Hey, are you with the guy you were singing with?" he asked.

Cass hesitated. She didn't want to give this guy any encouragement so she just nodded, hoping that would keep him from hitting on her.

The guy passed the joint he was smoking and Cass took it. "You two sounded good up there. Wow, how do you know Jesse?"

Cass shrugged. "Met him here." She thought she sounded very sophisticated.

Then she asked, "Who is he?"

"One of the best of the singers, musicians,

songwriters in the Bay Area." Then he looked at her closely. "You didn't know who he was?"

"Well, I didn't know he was well-known."

"He's gonna' be famous someday. His songs are first rate. He teach you that song you sang? By the way, my name is Joe."

She nodded in answer to his question, told him her name and then turned to the stage as a new person began singing. She decided to concentrate on the guy on stage.

After a while Joe moved on and Jesse came back in the coffee house minus Kayak.

"How'd it go? Forget your words?" he smiled as he kissed her lips in a quick peck.

Cass was taken by surprise, was sure she blushed, but had it together enough to kiss him back.

"Ummm...You're liking my kisses." He gazed at her intensely.

Cass tossed her head. "I can take 'um or leave 'um," she quipped.

Jesse laughed. "Let's go back to my boat. I've got something I want to show you."

"You have a boat?" Cass asked.

"My pad. I live on it."

Cass wanted to see his pad but she knew she was putting herself in a compromising position. However, she put her guitar away in its case and followed him down the gangplank to the pier.

After walking a few hundred yards down the dock, Jesse stepped onto a large sailboat, a 38-foot Hans

Christian. 'The Kayak' was painted on the stern. He helped her step aboard and led her to the cabin below. Kayak was waiting, wagging his tail at Jesse's entrance.

She gave Kayak several pats on the head and looked around at the attractive place. There was a bed in the far corner, a couch, table and chairs, all built in. Several guitars and other instruments rested against the walls of the interior. Recording equipment and speakers were stacked around the boat. There was incense burning and everything smelled of jasmine.

"What do you think of my mansion?" Jesse asked.

"Very nice…and cozy."

"Come sit here," he pointed to a couch.

Jesse went to a drawer and pulled out a bong and a chunk of dark substance that looked like hardened molasses.

"This is hash. You're gonna' love this."

He proceeded to break off a bit of the hash, crumbling it with his fingers as he put it in the bowl. He sprinkled a small amount of loose tobacco over the hash. He told her it was added to keep it burning. Then he poured water in the base of the bong and lit the bowl and began drawing the smoke from the crumbly, dark substance up through the stem.

"When you inhale, do it shallowly at first so you don't cough too much."

Cass took the bong and inhaled once. She began coughing immediately and handed it back to Jesse. When she caught her breath, she said, "That stuff is harsh."

"Let me show you." Jesse handed the pipe to her and as she placed her lips on the stem he said, "Just inhale a tiny bit. Hold it and then let out your breath."

Cass did what he said, and she didn't cough this time. After the second hit she was getting really stoned.

"This is quite strong," she said, giving Jesse a big grin.

Jesse took the bong from her hands and set it on the table. He put his arms around her shoulders and pulled her over to his side of the couch. Leaning toward her he kissed her on her lips. She liked the feeling and so she let him kiss and fondle her. But after a few minutes her mind interfered with her sensual feelings. She pulled herself upright and stood up. Once on her feet she felt dizzy and put her hand out to steady her balance.

"Feeling dizzy?" asked Jesse.

"Kind of."

Jesse stood, put his arm around her waist and walked her to the small refrigerator. He opened it and pulled out a bottle of white wine. Pulling the cork out with his teeth he poured wine into two glasses with his free hand.

Releasing her waist, he handed one glass to her and picked up the other one. "Here's to our friendship."

Cass pulled away and sat on the couch taking a small sip of wine. Her head was spinning but she felt great. Kayak came to sit beside her and looked up with big eyes.

"Even my dog is coming under your spell. What are you, a witchy woman?" Jesse asked.

Cass drank her wine and leaned back into the cushions of the couch. "Not sure what I am, but I feel good about it."

Jesse sat next to her and took some more hits off the bong. When he offered it, Cass shook her head. She was so stoned, she wasn't sure she could walk back to the boat.

Jesse put a record on the turntable. The sounds of Bob Dylan filled the small cabin. Candles were burning on the counter. When Jesse took her wine glass and set it on the table, he began kissing her again. She was fast succumbing to the bliss of it all. She went with her feelings this time and soon all her clothes were off and she was having sex with Jesse. Her mind was flying out into the universe. There were flying white horses and pink fluffy clouds. The sexual sensations were more intense than she'd ever experienced before. She laid back and enjoyed the sensual trip. Jesse kissed her everywhere, places she had never been kissed before. He was gentle but persistent and soon she felt a great explosion happening between her thighs. Jesse entered her and very quickly experienced his own explosion.

Next thing she was aware of, she was sitting up putting her clothes back on. Jesse was sitting in his underwear lighting a joint.

"Next lesson for you is dropping some acid. But not today. Enough of the stimulants for now. Let's go back to The Ark. The real music is about to start."

They finished the joint, Jesse dressed and they stepped off the sailboat and headed for the coffee house.

3

Jean Bartok was a large man, of Hungarian origin, spoke several languages, including French, Spanish, Basque, Greek, and Turkish, as well as English.

His penetrating blue eyes seduced many a damsel and angered some macho men. He could stop you in your tracks with his eyes, almost as if he had magical powers. The flowered Hawaiian shirts that he always wore were known around Sausalito. His fine paintings and collages were collected from Paris to New York to Mexico. Bartok's houseboat, the Valley-Ho lived in the slip next to Jesse's sailboat. He was not a musician but he had been a professional ballet dancer in his life, as well as a circus performer, set decorator, and actor. He was also a world-famous artist. Music was very important in his life.

Now in his sunset years, he still sailed to Mexico regularly and could drink most men under the table. He too, was a fixture on the Van Damme.

Cass was sitting at a table on deck drying her just-washed hair. Bartok came up the gangplank like a giant ready to take on any comers. His fierce countenance frightened a lot of people, but he was usually thinking of something sweet like the last woman he seduced, or the purple flowers he'd just picked down by the landing.

Bartok advanced toward Cass and she looked surprised.

"May I know the name of this glorious lady sitting in the sun?" he asked in his booming voice as he came to a stop in front of her.

"Uh…Cass."

"Mine is Bartok." He held out his huge hand.

Cass was somewhat unsure, but she put her small hand in his. He closed it and hers disappeared completely.

"I live next door," he shouted, as he released her hand. Some thought Bartok was hard of hearing.

"Cool," Cass said, quietly.

"What brings you to this den of iniquity, sweet lady?"

"I'm visiting."

"From where?"

"Los Angeles."

"Welcome to the San Francisco Bay Area where creativity blooms and eccentricity spirals."

Cass smiled at that. She liked this new man.

"Is Howard around," Bartok asked looking around the deck.

"I believe he's in the wheel house," Cass offered.

Bartok turned toward the cabin. "But I happen to know he's in there with a girl," Cass said, "so I think he probably doesn't want to be bothered."

"And how lass, would you know that?"

"Because the girl he is with is my friend. We came up from L.A. together."

Bartok leaned back and gave a great roar of a laugh.

"If I want to know anything about this boat I know who to ask."

Howard may have heard Bartok's loud voice or guffaw for the next moment he came out the wheel house door bare-chested, followed by Lia who was zipping up her pedal-pushers.

"My friend, how's it going today," Bartok offered his hand as was considered good manners in Bartok's generation.

Howard returned the hand shake. "Bitchin', Bartok. You?"

Bartok nodded and pulled Howard away from Lia and Cass. When he had him out of earshot, he said, "I've got some New York buyers coming out here and they need a place to stay so they can review my work on the boat. Could you put them up here? They have money and will pay whatever you asked, I'm sure."

Howard rubbed his chin. "I don't have anything fancy. What kind of digs you need?"

"It should be kind of nice. Anything you can fix up for them?"

Howard thought a minute. "I guess we can pick up some used furniture from the Salvation Army and a good bed and fix up something presentable."

Bartok face split into a big smile. "Can you have it ready this weekend?"

Howard nodded.

"Thanks, brother." Bartok slapped Howard on the back.

Howard coughed and turned to Lia. "Honey, this is Jean Bartok, our famous Gate Six artist in residence."

Bartok's eyes lit up and he bowed to Lia as he took her hand and kissed it. "It's a pleasure, my lady."

Lia smiled and glanced over at Cass who was smiling, too.

"Now Bartok, this is my girl, so hands off," Howard said good-naturedly.

"Of course, Captain. Never crossed my mind." Bartok smiled broadly.

"I'll get some of the guys together and we'll have the stateroom fixed up by Saturday," Howard said.

I'll bring them over when they arrive," Bartok said as he headed for the gangplank.

⌒

That Friday, Howard, John, Jesse and several of the guys who hung out at the boat began runs to the local Salvation Army Shop bringing a double bed, a couch, chair, and a couple of tables onto the boat. Howard chose a room at the top of the stairs, on deck, and it began to look like a pretty nice place. The walls were peeling but they did their best to pull off the paper and make it presentable. Lia and Cass hung some pictures of Bartok's on the walls. The floor was wood and uneven and splitting in places. Lia found old throw rugs and laid a couple across the worst of the splitting. The community head was just outside the room so they didn't have far to go. Lia and Cass began cleaning the room, set some fresh flowers in a vase, made up the bed with new sheets and a bedspread purchased at the Salvation Army store.

Bartok was excited at the prospect of the New York buyers picking up some of his paintings. He'd had shows in New York, Mexico City and Paris at different times, but lately he'd let his marketing slide. He had no agent so he arranged for the shows himself. He was more interested in painting and creating than marketing, as many artists are, so his financial status had suffered. When he noticed his bank account getting low, he contacted some friends at a gallery in New York and they found the buyers that were interested enough to fly out to see Bartok's work.

Bartok borrowed Howard's van and picked up the Cohen's at the airport. Around 3 p.m. he showed up at the boat with his guests.

Cass saw a man and woman in their 60s step from the van. She was over-dressed, New York style, wearing lots of eye-makeup, a tight-fitting outfit and he had on a white linen suit and Panama hat. They boarded the Charles Van Damme, leaning a bit with the listing of the ship. Howard was there to greet them.

"Welcome, Mr. and Mrs. Cohen," Howard said, extending his hand.

Mr. Cohen took his hand and Mrs. Cohen dipped her head.

"My friend and Captain of this ship, Howard is your host," Bartok said, to his guests, as he struggled with two suitcases.

Howard showed them to a couple of deck chairs. "Would you like a drink? Water, Scotch, Whiskey?" Howard offered.

"Thanks, we'll have a Scotch," Mr. Cohen said.

Lia and Cass moved away so the four could talk business.

Howard went inside the coffee house and poured four glasses of Glenlivet, bringing them back on a tray. He set two before the Cohen's, one in front of Bartok and kept one for himself.

"We have a room ready for you," said Howard. "I'm sorry it isn't the best accommodations, but for a dry-docked boat it's pretty nice."

"We appreciate your putting us up," Mr. Cohen said.

"Could you point me toward the restroom," Mrs. Cohen asked.

Howard waved Lia over. "Lia, show Mrs. Cohen the room and the head."

Lia and Cass took Mrs. Cohen aft to the room that had been fixed up.

When she stepped inside, she took in the walls and the floor. Her mouth dropped but she said nothing. "Thank you, girls," she said. Lia pointed out the head outside in the hall and they left Mrs. Cohen.

Lia and Cass returned to the main deck and saw that Mr. Cohen and Howard had gone into the Coffee House. Bartok was nowhere to be seen. Howard was pouring more Scotch for Mr. Cohen.

"Want something to drink, girls?" Howard asked.

Lia and Cass shook their heads.

Mr. Cohen continued his conversation. "I want to purchase several of Bartok's paintings and collages to take back to New York. We just bought a new house in Scarsdale and I want to hang them in our place and sell some of them to friends."

"There are two of his works hanging in the room you will be sleeping in," Howard said. "He has many more on his houseboat which is just a few steps away."

"Yes," Mr. Cohen continued. "As soon as we rest up, maybe tomorrow I want to take a look."

"By the way, what do you want for putting us up?" Mr. Cohen took out his wallet.

"Oh, twenty dollars for the night would be good," Howard said.

Mr. Cohen looked shocked. "Heavens, no." He peeled off a one hundred dollar bill from his wallet and handed it to Howard. "I think we'll only be here one night, but I'll give you more if we stay longer."

Howard took the money and slipped it into his pocket, thanking Mr. Cohen.

Cass and Lia exchanged glances. Cass picked up her guitar and started to leave.

"Where you off to?" Lia asked.

"I'm going down to my room and practice the new song Jesse taught me."

"Okay, see you later."

That night Jesse came late; Cass had already sung a few songs in the early part of the evening. The Cohen's were sitting down front having a drink. Howard kept the Heroin and Cocaine out of sight. He cautioned the musicians NOT to bring any white stuff on board. Howard told them smoking pot was okay. He figured they shouldn't have to change their complete life style for a couple of wealthy New Yorkers and perspective buyers of Bartok's art work. Neither Mr. nor Mrs. Cohen took notice of the marijuana smoke permeating the air. Cass even thought she heard a giggle or two from Mrs. Cohen. She probably got a contact high from breathing the heavy smoke-laden air.

At midnight the Cohen's took their leave and went to their *stateroom*. Then the dishes of white stuff came out and the dollar bills appeared. Howard used his new one-hundred dollar bill to snort the coke, but did not leave it on the table.

Jesse sat beside Cass and held her hand. When the coke was passed, both of them snorted a couple of lines. Then Jesse joined his fellow musicians, David, John, Spence and they jammed all night long.

Cass finally left around 3 a.m. and crawled into her bunk, pushing the trunk in place across the door. She had just fallen asleep when there was a knock at the door.

"Cass, its Jesse."

She rubbed her eyes, got out of bed and went to the door pulling the trunk away.

Jesse slipped inside the room and pulled her into his arms. He kissed her long and hard.

He back-walked her to the bunk and they fell on it.

After a few more kisses, he pulled off his shirt and pants and climbed in beside her.

Cass was taken by surprise at his visit; she hadn't expected him to come find her. He didn't say anything upstairs. How did he know she didn't have another guy in bed with her? That's the way things happened around this boat. Spur of the moment things.

4

$\mathcal{L}$ia stretched as the morning light filtered between the shades Howard had erected across the large windows of the wheel house. She reached her legs across the bed to feel Howard's body, but he was not in bed. She turned over and sat up; noticing Howard was nowhere to be seen. Finding her clothes in a pile on the floor she got dressed in yesterday's green pedal-pushers and green tee-shirt, ran Howard's comb through her long blond hair, and stepped out the door on deck. Howard was sitting at the table with a cup of coffee in his hand.

"Hey sleepy head." He greeted her.

She rubbed her eyes. "Any more of that coffee?"

Howard rose and went to the coffee house galley and came back out with a steaming cup in his hand.

Lia sat with him at the wooden picnic table and drank her coffee in silence. The morning sun was quite warm, the usual sea breeze gently blowing.

"What's happening today," Lia asked.

"I've got to fix a few things on the top deck. Need to run down to the hardware store in town and get some parts. Want to come along? We could have lunch in town."

Lia nodded. She loved walking around Sausalito and checking out the clothing shops. They were pretty expensive but she could sometimes find sales.

She hadn't realized how emotionally connected Howard was becoming until last night when they made love. He had said to her in the heat of passion that he was divorcing his wife, Faye, and he and Lia could get hitched if she wanted. She had one more year at UCLA before graduation and she hadn't figured on getting married, to anyone. He knew she had an inheritance from her family in Germany and never had to worry about money. Howard had a small savings account he had accumulated from his last job as an engineer and that was what he lived on right now. She didn't know if she loved him but she certainly was crazy about him.

They finished their coffee. "Ready to go into town?" Howard asked.

"I need to wash up first." She went into the head next to the wheel house, peeled off her clothes, and jumped in the shower. After drying off, she walked naked around the corner to the wheel house and found her suitcase, slipped on a pair of shorts and a clean tee-shirt. Running Howard's comb through her hair again she walked out to the table and joined him.

"That was fast," he said.

Lia shrugged and smiled.

She and Howard walked hand in hand down the gangplank, climbed into Lia's MG and headed for town.

⌐

Sausalito in the 1960s was an upscale community with a lot of money, gorgeous houses, condos, and luxurious apartments, built on the side of the hills. Below the million dollar homes a lovely yacht harbor nestled in a cove between the Golden Gate Bridge and Angel Island. Further along the inland beach of Sausalito, a community of house boats and vessels were anchored to assorted docks. This was where Gate Six was located; where the Van Damme Boat found its home.

The town had a colorful history; During World War II, Fort Barry and Fort Baker were staging areas for American troops. After the war, the houseboat community grew up along the waterfront, housing a few famous musicians, actors and assorted artists. One of the more infamous characters of Sausalito was Sally Stanford, former city council member, mayor of the town, and founder of the restaurant Valhalla. She was also well-known for a brothel in San Francisco on Pine Street. Downtown Sausalito was comprised of a few blocks of expensive shops and gift stores, restaurants and coffee houses.

The hippie movement was just coming into its glory in 1963. Folk music had been the primary motivator of musicians in California and especially on the San Francisco scene, but some of the musicians were branching out and adding some rockabilly music to their songs. Dylan, Baez, and Simon and Garfunkel were the big draws, musically, but The Beach Boys music was taking the west coast by storm with their surfing sounds. Then Surf Rock emerged as well as Hot Rod Rock with its revving engines and screeching tires. Bo Diddley blues, drugs and getting high became prevalent in the lifestyle of the San Francisco scene; this having a lot to do with the influences on the music.

Lia drove into the lot beside the park in downtown Sausalito. She and Howard walked to the hardware store where he bought some parts for the galley and then headed across the street to the Tides Book Store and Coffee Shop. Lia browsed in the books while Howard bought a paper and read it. Then they ordered lunch at the coffee shop.

Howard folded the paper and began to eat. "I want to pick up some weed before we go back to the boat. That okay with you?"

"Where?" Lia asked.

"Not far from here. I can leave you here and take the car and go get it myself." He knew she was nervous about getting busted for buying weed. The authorities usually didn't bother with marijuana sales, but you could never be sure the seller wasn't being watched.

"Why don't you do that," Lia said. "I'll do some shopping while you're gone."

Lia noticed an attractive brunette wearing a long granny dress, enter the book store. She looked around and spotted Lia and Howard. Lia saw her eyes widen and then she headed right for their table. Lia nudged Howard and nodded toward the woman coming in their direction with an apparent attitude.

"Oh shit," Howard said under his breath.

She stopped at the table and slapped Howard on

the right side of his face. He jumped up, grabbed her arms and pushed her down in the place where he had been sitting.

"Son of a bitch, Faye, don't make a scene. They'll throw us out or call the cops."

The other customers were looking but it was a familiar scene in the Bay Area.

The lovely brunette glared at Lia across the table. "I don't give a shit. How dare you appear in public with your mistress."

Lia was ready to make a quick exit, but Howard, standing between the women at the side of the table, held her down gently with a hand on her arm.

"No reason to get bent out of shape, Faye." He looked at the two women. "Faye, this is Lia, Lia this is my wife, Faye."

Faye continued to glare at Lia and wouldn't speak to her. Lia remained silent, thinking this was the best course of action.

"Why haven't you called or come home? You've been gone for days. I know you're running the coffee house on the boat but I thought you'd come home during the daytime." Faye blurted this out and then hiccupped as tears ran down her cheeks.

Howard patted her back. "I've been busy with the boat. I have to fix all the problems that occur. Right now we're in town to get parts for the galley."

"Yeah, I can see you've been busy." She scowled at Lia and glowered at her husband.

"Look I'll try to get over in a few days. How are the kids?"

"What do you care? You never have time for them anymore."

Faye finally gave in and started sobbing. Lia took this opportunity to slip out of the booth, gesture to Howard she would be out on the street and headed for the door.

Jesus! Just what she needed. To run into an irate wife! Howard had told her his wife was ambivalent as to what he did. Apparently he told her a fib. Actually he'd lied to her, Lia told herself. And all that baloney about getting a divorce. Didn't look like Faye knew anything about Howard filing for divorce. Probably lied about that, too.

She walked over to the parking lot, got into her MG and drove away. To hell with him. He could get back to the boat on his own. Maybe she'd just pack up and leave.

5

Jesse stepped on his boat, went to the cabin and fed a hungry Kayak. He hadn't come home last night, having stayed with Cass and his dog had missed him. However, before Kayak ate from his bowl he jumped into Jesse's arms and they wrestled a bit. When Kayak had had enough rough-house he bent down to eat his food.

Jesse thought about Cass. She was a very lovely girl, and still somewhat innocent in spite of being married five years. He liked her honesty and her love of music. She was fun and good company. He'd keep her as a girlfriend for the summer. After that, who knew? He couldn't make plans very far ahead.

His parents were appearing in a circus in nearby Napa in the next couple of weeks. He hadn't been in contact with them; he'd seen it on a poster. He had thought of borrowing a car and going up there. It had been a couple of years since he'd seen them. He had a love-hate relationship with them. Loving them didn't mean he wanted to be around them for very long. His parents had a trapeze act in the Winter Brothers Circus that traveled the United States. He had met Bartok in the same circus when he traveled with them as a trapeze performer. Jesse was a kid then. He couldn't wait to get away and start his own life. He'd bought his boat when he sold his first song to the Kingston Trio. He never regretted it and the royalties gave him a steady income. This song that the Kingston

Trio recorded went to the top of the charts.

When he moored at Gate Six next to the Van Damme boat, he met Howard and they became friends.

Howard had told Jesse he had met Faye at an all night jam several years ago, fell for her, got her pregnant and married her because she insisted. His wife lived in an apartment with the kids in San Francisco and he lived here where he could have a free and easy life style. He visited his family once every week or so, but his life was that of a single man living on the boat.

Then one serendipitous afternoon, Howard introduced Jesse to the local Gate Six artist, Bartok, and they both recognized each other. He didn't want to be reminded that his sister had fallen from the trapeze and was in a wheel chair. He knew his father had pushed her to do something nearly impossible, the bastard, and she'd fallen! Maybe he should stay away from them. They had such intense auras and powerful personalities. He'd think about it. If he went, maybe he would take Cass with him.

Jesse showered, changed his clothes and took Kayak for a walk. He ended up at the Kettle Deli, tied Kayak to the bicycle rack and went inside. Cass was in the back eating a sandwich and reading a book.

"Hi, can I join you?"

Cass looked up. "Sure." She closed her book and continued eating.

Jesse ordered a sandwich and a beer. "Been practicing the song I taught you?"

"Yes, I have. I've got it mostly together."

"Good. Will you sing it tonight?"

"I'm still working on the chords. Maybe you could help me."

"Sure. We'll go back to the boat after lunch and I'll show you some simple chords.

I'll be glad to play it for you tonight."

Cass smiled. "I'd love that."

"I have a friend coming who wants to hear the song."

"Oh no, I'm not singing it for some outsider. I don't know the words that well, yet."

"Relax, he's not an outsider. He's interested in recording the song and I couldn't think of a better songbird to sing it than you. And what you do is write the words on a small piece of paper and stick it on the side of your guitar. It's called a cheat sheet."

Cass wasn't convinced. "I don't know if I can do it, Jesse."

"Of course you can. I'll be up there on stage with you."

They finished their food, and Jesse left money on the table.

"If you keep paying for my lunches I'll have to start paying you back."

"I'll just take it out in trade, girl." Jesse gave her a big smile. "Let's go back and practice *Moanin' Blues*.

Cass smiled back but didn't feel totally comfortable at his remark.

They exited the Kettle Deli and went back to the Van Damme.

⤶

That night in The Ark, the Cohens were in the front row again. Al Cohen had bought about twenty paintings and collages of Bartok and had them shipped to New York. Both he and Bartok were very happy with the deal. Bartok had realized approximately $75,000 from the sale and he was flying high without stimulants. Al knew he could sell most of them for triple what he'd paid and was elated, too.

Cass was the second performer to take the stage. Jesse sat on a stool and she stood before the mike, obviously nervous.

Jesse winked at her and whispered, "Be cool, girl. Nothing to fear."

Jesse's friend was sitting down front and it made Cass doubly anxious. Jesse started playing and Cass joined him singing the lyrics. They harmonized on the chorus and the minor notes wafted across the coffee house. Cass's pure high voice and Jesse's low register mingled like the music of a summer's rain in the trees.

After they finished, the applause was heavier than usual. When Cass and Jesse left the stage, he guided her over to the guy at a front table.

"Paul, this is my friend, Cass."

The tall man stood up and shook her hand. "You have a lovely voice. You two sound great together." He pulled out a chair for Cass and she thanked him for the compliment.

Jesse sat on the other side of Paul.

"Paul owns a little recording studio in Berkeley. I

taught Cass the song so she would have something new in her repertoire."

Paul was drinking a glass of wine and Jesse poured two more glasses from the bottle on the table for Cass and himself.

"Well, what do you think about the song?" Jesse asked.

Paul nodded. "I got a new artist who needs some new songs. Sorry I'm not offering to record you singing it. But I'll pay you a good amount for it."

Cass stood up and started to leave as they were talking business, but Jesse pulled her back down in her chair.

"What will you pay?"

"I'll pay fifty dollars," Paul said.

Jesse looked astonished. "No way! That song has potential. How about $100?"

Paul shook his head. "I'll give you $75 and that's my final offer."

Jesse was silent for a few minutes, then turned to Paul and said, "Nope, it's for sale for $100 or you don't get it."

Cass was swept with unfamiliar emotions. She felt Jesse expected more money for the song and she was sad for him that he didn't get it.

Paul took out a wad of bills and peeled off $100. "Can you give me the words and music so I can take it back to the musician?"

Jesse nodded. "I'll go get a copy of the music and lyrics on my boat. It will just take a minute."

Cass started to rise again, and Jesse pushed her down gently. "Wait here for me."

She was supposed to talk with this dude that had just ripped off Jesse, Cass thought.

When Jesse was gone, Cass didn't stop to think, she blurted out, "You know his song is worth more than $100."

Paul looked at her in amazement. "And how would you know, little girl?"

"I just know. He could make a lot more money with another producer." Cass was getting braver.

Paul laughed out loud. "I can't imagine why you would say that. Aren't you a friend of Jesse's?"

"I am. That's why I said that and I think you know it's true. If I were you I wouldn't want the public to know I took advantage of a down-and-out musician. Did I mention I was a newspaper correspondent in L.A.?"

Paul looked more carefully at Cass. He didn't think that kind of publicity would be good for his client who would record the song. Maybe he should rethink the sale.

"Well, maybe we can talk more about the price when Jesse returns," Paul offered.

Jesse came back up the ramp with papers in his hand. He sat down next to Cass and slid the written music across to Paul.

"Uh…Cass has convinced me that I didn't pay you enough for the song. So I'm going to give you $300. Does that suit you?"

Jesse looked from Cass to Paul. "I guess so. Uh…sure."

Paul reached in his vest and pulled out a wallet. He counted out $200 and handed it over to Jesse. "I don't want you trying to sue me now for not paying enough money for this song."

"No, of course not," Jesse said with a big smile.

"Cass," Paul looked at her, "You won't be able to sing this song once my artist releases his album, without paying a fee to me, because I own the song."

"That won't happen," Jesse said. "Cass can sing that song anytime she wants and I don't want you to try and stop her with any legal action."

Paul knew when he was whipped. "Okay, just this one song. Gotta' go now. Any more songs you want to sell, give me a call," Paul said, eyeing Cass again.

When Paul was down the gangplank and out of earshot, Jesse turned to Cass. "What the hell did you say to him?"

"I just reminded him that the song was worth a lot more than $100. I reminded him it wouldn't be cool to let the public know he ripped off a struggling musician. He finally agreed. I guess I didn't tell you I used to be a newspaper correspondent in L.A." She smiled up at him with an impish grin.

"Girl, I think I need to hire you for negotiations from now on when selling my music." He squeezed her shoulder and gave her a kiss on the cheek. "No, you didn't tell me you were a reporter."

"I used to work for the Los Angeles Times. Quit after my divorce. I needed some R & R. And I'd be happy to help with your negotiations," Cass said, kissing him back on the mouth.

6

$\mathcal{H}$oward was pissed at Faye's display of temper and jealousy in the Tides Coffee Shop. He finally got Faye calmed down, sent her on her way, and went out on the sidewalk looking for Lia. Her MG was gone from the parking lot. He hiked back to the boat and found her packing.

"Look, babe, I'm sorry that happened. I thought Faye understood since we lived apart that we were over. I try to support her and the kids but it's hard when you don't have a job."

Lia kept slamming clothes in her suitcase trying to ignore him.

Finally Howard grabbed her arms and made her look at him. "Lia, I care about YOU, I want you to stay. We'll sort this out and decide what to do with our future."

"What future? You already have a family. We don't have a future."

"We do, girl. I promise you. I'll get a job when this summer is over. By that time my savings will have almost run out. I'll divorce Faye and we can be together."

Lia looked up at him with wet eyes. "I have one more year of college at UCLA. I can't stay here after the summer."

"You can go to college here, in Berkeley," Howard insisted.

Lia looked at him. "Howard, this is a summer fling. Get used to it." But she let him take her in his arms and begin kissing her. Soon their clothes were off and they were on the bed. He murmured all the things he had before, and she tried not to listen.

Afterwards he held her in his arms tightly. She felt at peace in spite of their argument. Maybe she'd stay after all for the summer. She had no other plans and she was sure Cass was not ready to go back to L.A.

Howard breathed a sigh of relief having avoided losing his summer girlfriend. He'd be more careful about her feelings. She wasn't as committed to him as he'd thought.

⤳

Faye drove fast back to her apartment in the Mission district of San Francisco. She kept wiping away the tears so she could see to drive. Damn Howard! She knew he was unfaithful from time to time but she didn't think he'd have a girlfriend. She didn't know how to get back at him except to keep the children away from him but he didn't seem to want to see them very often as it was. She'd think of something to punish him. Maybe she'd just show up on the boat and move into the wheel house. Throw out the tramp's clothes if any were there. That would piss Howard off and create a scene in front of his friends.

She pulled into her parking spot in the garage and walked up to her 4th floor apartment. Carol the babysitter was reading on the couch.

"Thanks, Carol for coming on such short notice." She handed her money and the girl smiled and left.

Howie and Nancy were down for their afternoon nap. Howie was four and Nancy three. She thought back to the beginning of their romance. She had gotten pregnant and she insisted Howard marry her. He had never really lived with them, preferring to reside somewhere else. He did pay the rent and utilities and gave her money for food, which she knew was a drain on his savings, but damn it, he owed it to her. He'd saddled her with two children and he lived as if he were free and single. She knew he wasn't committed to her or the children but she loved him anyway.

She folded some clothes on the bed and then lay down for a good cry.

⟿

"Why did you tell me your wife didn't mind you having girlfriends?" Lia asked. She and Howard were sitting on the bed smoking a joint.

"I really thought she was resigned to our being apart. I give her money every month but we haven't slept together for two years. I do that to take care of the kids, but I told her when they get in school I expect her to get a job."

Lia thought about what Howard had said and decided it wasn't entirely his fault. "She obviously doesn't want to turn loose of you or she wouldn't be jealous," Lia said.

"I guess."

"When will you file for divorce?"

"Soon, babe, soon. You need to make arrangements to transfer to U.C. Berkeley before it's too late to get in."

Lia contemplated changing schools. Did she really want to transfer to Berkeley? She'd still have to return to L.A. to get her things and move out of her studio apartment. And Cass needed to return at the end of the summer.

She nodded distractedly as Howard was talking about looking for work himself when the summer was over.

Meanwhile she had the rest of the summer to enjoy the boat, lovely Sausalito and Howard, not necessarily in that order.

7

Jesse was sitting on deck of his boat playing the guitar. He saw Cass coming down the dock. She stepped into the boat and sat down next to him. "Are you coming over to The Ark? Howard is planning a party to celebrate Bartok's sales of his paintings and your sales of the song."

"Sure. When?"

"Right now. Lia and I just baked four carrot cakes, and Howard went out and bought Tequila, Scotch and Vodka plus some chips, and snacks."

"Bitchin', that should last us awhile."

"Howard said it would be an all-night party."

"Let's get it on, then." He packed up his guitar in its case and called to Kayak.

Jesse and Cass left the boat with Kayak trailing behind and headed for The Ark.

Jesse was thinking about how he really felt about Cass. He liked her a lot, in fact, enough so he hadn't balled any other girls since she arrived on the scene. That was unusual for him. But he was opposed to sticking to one girl as it went against his basic instincts. However, there hadn't been anyone else who caught his eye. Maybe he should look more carefully at the audience when they jammed at night. Groupies always hung around for hours listening to the music. He felt he might be in some danger of liking Cass more than he wanted to.

When he and Cass arrived at The Ark several people were already there. Food was piled on the tables in the coffee house along with plates of Cocaine, weed and several assorted pipes. Vodka and Scotch bottles and paper cups were in view for the taking.

"Want to do some coke?" Jesse asked Cass.

She shook her head. "Not right now, maybe later."

Jesse went over and snorted up while a line formed behind him. Cass vowed to write about this scene later in her journal. It was something she didn't want to forget, it was so bizarre.

Bartok came over. "Hello dear Cass. Where have you been keeping yourself?" Then he looked at Jesse as he returned to Cass's side. "I'm thinking I know the answer."

Lia and Howard came out of the wheel house and joined the crowd. Howard poured cups of Scotch for him and Lia and they queued up for the Cocaine line.

Soon more musicians arrived and began tuning up together and playing their instruments. Jesse joined the group and left Cass with Kayak lying beside her.

Joe came over and sat beside Cass. Kayak growled quietly.

Cass laughed. "Looks like Kayak is looking out for me," she said.

"Hey Kayak. No harm intended here. Just a little conversation," Joe protested.

"Are you going to sing tonight?"

"I don't know. Probably not, except with the group."

People began dancing to the music. "Want to dance?" Joe asked Cass.

"No thanks. I don't think Kayak will let me," she joked.

"Boy, that Jesse has his dog well trained. It's like Kayak understands that no one is to get too close to you."

"I'm as surprised as you," Cass said.

"Ok. I'm gonna' look for another chick that doesn't have a dog attached." Joe waved and left.

A while later the musicians took a break. Jesse came over. "Who was the guy making a pass at you?"

"Just a guy that hangs out on the boat."

"What did he want?"

"He wanted to dance. You sound jealous."

"Naw, not me." Jesse grinned as he took a swig of her Scotch.

"If I'd wanted to dance I would have. Kayak growled and he left."

Jesse laughed. "Kayak's protecting my interests." At the sound of his name he sat up and licked Jesse's hand.

Jesse poured more Scotch into Cass cup. He took her hand and stood up.

He pulled her up and they went over to the Cocaine table. "Want some now?"

"Sure." Cass snorted a couple of lines through a straw. Jesse did the same. The sensation still stung her nostrils and numbed her throat but made her body feel lovely. She could smell the aroma of freshly ground coffee beans wafting across the room. Jesse stopped to pour coffee on top of the Scotch.

"Where are the Cohens?" Jesse asked.

"They went to the city to see friends. Aren't coming back until late," Cass said.

"That's good. Bartok won't get freaked out because of the Cocaine on the tables."

The musicians were headed back on stage to resume their playing. Jesse kissed Cass and she went back to her seat by Kayak. She noticed a young girl run up on stage and hug Jesse and talked to him in an animated manner. He talked to her for a few minutes smiling at her. When he turned to begin playing she left the stage and sat right down in front.

The party went on all day and all night. Cass stayed there until two in the morning. She slipped out of the coffee house and went to her bunk, slipped her shorts and top off and climbed into bed. She didn't push the trunk against the door thinking maybe Jesse would come down when the party broke up.

The next morning she awoke and Jesse was not beside her.

8

$\mathcal{B}$artok put down his paint brush and took a drink of Scotch. The Cohens had left that morning; Bartok had borrowed Howards VW van and drove them to the airport and they agreed to return when he had more paintings to show them.

He crammed a handful of potato chips into his mouth and stepped back to view his work. Not bad, he said to himself. He loved to create bay scenes, with sail boats, the city of San Francisco in the background with the Golden Gate Bridge. Often they would evolve into an abstraction and the bridge or sail boats were hardly recognizable. Today he was laying the paint on the canvas in an impasto style. He threw in a couple of washers and a playing card or two. A few more found objects went into his composition. He would step back often and look at his work. His parrot Helen would sing opera along with the record Bartok had on the phonograph. *Carmina Burana*, wafted across the docks of Gate Six, over the tops of houseboats and all the way to The Ark.

Bartok would do a little dance around his houseboat as he twisted his brush into the paint. Finally he decided it was finished. He took it out on deck in the brilliant light and looked approvingly at his art work. Another piece for sale, he thought happily. He stacked it in a safe place for the oils to dry, wiped his hands on a grimy rag, and downed the rest of the Scotch.

He'd really tied one on last night. The best medicine was a bit of the hair of the dog, meaning a glass of
Scotch this morning. The guys were still playing when
he crept; half crawled to his boat and climbed into his
bunk. He saw Cass leave and he noticed Jesse flirting
with the young blonde next to the stage. Good thing
he waited until Cass left. That would have been disre-
spectful to her if she'd seen him. But now days young
people didn't care about respect or commitment or
faithfulness. They just took their pleasure where they
found it and the consequences be Dammed. Couples
came together and broke apart all the time on The Ark.

9

$\mathcal{F}$aye hadn't slept well last night or any of the nights since she found Howard at the Tides with his girlfriend. She cried all the time and the kids kept asking what was wrong. She had this tight ball in her gut that was painful. Something in her throat threatened to close her esophagus and she couldn't get bites of food down. She was a mess.

It was Howard's fault. He took her for granted and thought he could throw her away like an old newspaper. She lay back on the bed and continued crying. Maybe she should shake him up a little. Show him she wasn't going to be a doormat anymore.

In the drawer beside the bed was a gun that Howard had given her a few years ago for protection since she was alone so much of the time. She opened the drawer and took out the gun, a 38 special. Checking the chamber she saw it was loaded. She threw on some clothes, called Carol, her babysitter, and walked to the living room and placed the gun in her large purse. She made coffee, toasted a piece of bread and waited for the door bell. Carol came over quickly.

"Fix the kids some breakfast. You can eat with them if you haven't."

Faye picked up her purse, grabbed a sweater from the hall closet and went downstairs to her car.

The day was cool in San Francisco, a slight breeze coming off the bay. Traffic was light on the Golden

Gate Bridge but all of this was lost on Faye. She had a single mission in mind.

᠊ᢁ

Cass walked down to Jesse's boat and noticed Kayak wagging his tail at her. Then she looked over by the boom at Jesse and the girl. Jesse's arm was around her.

Kayak gave a friendly bark at Cass and Jesse turned around. Cass backed away, turned and ran back down the dock to the Van Damme. By the time she was in her room she had wet cheeks. She pushed the trunk in place against the door and lay on the bunk. Soon there was knocking on the door. She heard Jesse's voice.

"Cass, let me in."

"Go away."

"Let me explain."

"No."

"Ok. If you want to talk I'll be up on deck for a while."

After that, it was quiet except for Cass's crying.

When the tears dried, she got up, combed her hair and put some moisturizer on her cheeks. She pulled the trunk away and went up on deck. Jesse was sitting at a table in the Coffee House talking to Howard and Lia. She went over to the table and sat down next to Lia.

Jesse gave her a warm smile. "We were just talking about a sailing trip on the bay in my boat today. Interested in coming along?" He looked straight at Cass.

"Maybe."

"I'll fix some sandwiches and we'll take some Scotch," Lia commented.

"Sounds good," Cass said.

"The wind is good, not too brisk," Jesse said.

"When do you plan to shove off?" Howard asked.

"As soon as we get organized," Jesse said.

"I'll go fix some food. Cass, come with me." Lia stood up and started for the galley.

At that moment, they all saw Faye storm up the gangplank and head for the group at the table.

"Oh, God," Howard exclaimed.

He tried to head her off by going to meet her.

"You bastard!" she screamed. "You can't just throw me over. I'm your wife and I have rights." Faye was working herself into a hysterical fit. She pulled a gun from her purse and started waving it around.

Jesse grabbed Cass with one hand and Lia with the other and headed in the other direction for the stairs to the lower deck.

Lia tried to pull away. "No," she said, "I need to stay with Howard."

"You come with us. It's Howard's fight, not yours."

They dashed down to the next deck and into Cass's room. Jesse pulled the trunk in place and led the two girls over to the bunk.

"My God! Do you think she will hurt Howard?" asked Lia.

"I have no idea, but I thought we should get away from her," said Jesse.

"I'm sorry, Cass about this morning when the girl was on my boat," Jesse said. He slipped his arm around her waist. "I never said I was faithful. It meant nothing to me. I don't even know her name. I sent her on her way. Please give me another chance."

One part of Cass's brain was telling her, this is the standard line from a guy who wants back in your good graces or in your pants, as was the case here. The other part of her wanted to make up and let it go.

"Let's talk about it another time, Jesse. I'm worried about what's happening on deck."

Up on deck, Faye leveled the gun at Howard's chest. "I'll teach you a lesson. If I can't have you, neither can anyone else."

Howard put his hand out in front of him. "Faye, listen. Put the gun down. This is no way to resolve this." He stepped forward to disarm her and she pulled the trigger. Then she shot him a second time.

Howard fell to the deck. He cried out, "Faye, no."

Blood seeped from his chest and spread out beneath him. He lapsed into unconsciousness. Faye fell on her knees, dropped the gun on the deck and put her arms around Howard's waist with her head on his chest.

In the stillness of the lower deck the three heard a gunshot, then another. Then silence. Lia bolted for the door.

"No. Stay here." Jesse grabbed her by the wrist. "We don't need to get involved with a woman with a gun. We have no protection."

"But Howard might be hurt. Or they both might be." Lia was crying now.

"Listen, honey, we need to do what Jesse says. We can't be of any help right now." Cass was trying to comfort her friend.

Lia was sobbing, lying on the bunk.

There were no noises coming from up above, so Jesse pulled the trunk away from the door.

"You two stay here. I mean it. I'm going to sneak up the stairs and see what's going on."

Jesse left and Lia continued to cry while Cass sat beside her on the bunk.

Jesse peeked around the top of the stair. There was no one in sight. He crept toward the deck and then he saw them. Howard was lying on the deck and Faye was collapsed by his side crying with her head in her hands. The gun was lying beside her right hand. When Jesse got closer he saw all the blood under Howard's shoulder.

Bartok came charging up the gangplank. "What happened? I thought I heard gunshots."

He saw Howard and Faye and that answered everything. "Oh, my God," he murmured.

He and Jesse arrived at Howard's side at the same time. Jesse picked up the gun by the barrel and ran inside the Coffee House. He placed it on the counter. Then he ran back to Howard. Bartok leaned down and spoke.

"Howard, are you conscious?" he asked

No response from Howard.

"We need to call an ambulance," Jesse said.

"Yes, do that. I'll stay with Howard."

Faye was still crying beside Howard and she hadn't said a word.

Jesse sprinted down the gangplank to the nearest pay phone on the dock and called an ambulance and the Sausalito police. He ran back just in time to see Lia and Cass come up from below deck.

Lia ran to Howard's other side, and laid her hand on his forehead. She picked up a towel and laid it across his chest over the bullet hole.

Faye looked over at Lia. "Take your hands off him, you bitch." She yelled.

"You've killed him, you ass," Lia managed to say.

"He's my husband and I can do with him what I want." She made a lunge for Lia but Cass saw it coming and grabbed Faye by her hair. She landed on Howard's legs missing Lia.

Howard began moaning and Faye immediately leaned down and spoke to him. "I'm sorry honey. I didn't mean to hurt you. I was just so damn mad."

Lia continued to brush his brow lightly with her hand. This time Faye chose to ignore it. She put her head on Howard's shoulder. He moaned again.

"You're hurting him, Faye," Lia said.

Faye lifted her head and kissed him on the mouth. She sat up as the Sausalito police came running up the gangplank along with the ambulance attendants carrying a gurney.

"Move out of the way, ladies," One of the attendants said. They proceeded to slide Howard onto the gurney and carried him off the Van Damme to the ambulance.

One of the policemen spoke. "What occurred here?"

"This woman, Howard's wife shot him," Jesse said.

"Did you see her shoot him?" asked the cop.

"No, we were below deck. We had run away when she came on board," Jesse explained.

One of the policemen was holding Faye by the arm. "Where's the weapon?"

Jesse showed them where he had laid it on the counter.

"Did you touch it?" asked the first cop.

"I picked it up by the barrel," continued Jesse. "It was lying beside her when I came up on deck. I didn't want her to shoot me, so I took it out of her reach."

The cop holding Faye's arm said, "Ma'am, what is your name please?" There was still no response from Faye.

"Her name is Faye Bateman," Jesse said.

"I'll need your names and the victim's name and for all of you to come down to the station and sign statements." He looked at Lia who was still crying and Cass who had her arm around her waist.

"Who are you two ladies?"

"They are guests on the boat. We three were down stairs when we heard the gun shots," Jesse replied.

Bartok told them who he was and the four of them were herded into a police car. Faye was placed in another car and they all left for the police station.

At the station, Jesse explained what happened. Faye was still mute.

Lia told what occurred at the book store a few days before. She told them she was Howard's girlfriend and she thought Faye was not concerned about Howard's life on the boat.

They each signed a statement as to their version of what occurred and then they were released. The police placed Faye under arrest and kept her at the station. Faye still hadn't uttered a word.

"I have to go to the hospital. Where was Howard taken?" Lia asked the policeman at the desk.

"Marin General."

"I'll go with you," Cass said.

Outside the station the girls and Jesse and Bartok hailed a cab and had the driver take them to Marin General.

At the emergency desk Lia asked, "Did you just admit a Howard Bateman? He was shot on the Van Damme boat."

The attendant looked at the log and said, "He was just admitted. He's in surgery right now. Just take a seat and we'll let you know when he's out of surgery."

The four of them sat in the emergency lounge. Lia began crying again and Cass tried to comfort her.

"Never a dull minute on The Ark," Bartok quipped grimly.

"I'd just as soon it wasn't so action-packed," Jesse said.

The four of them waited for two hours before anyone came out to talk with them. Finally a doctor came out of the emergency room and looked around, slipping off his mask. "Relatives of Howard Bateman," he called.

"We're his friends, and this is his girlfriend," Jesse said, putting his arm around Lia. "We were with him when he was shot."

"The first bullet passed through his shoulder," the surgeon said. "The other bullet lodged very close to his heart. For now he's out of danger. You can see him in a little while."

Lia stopped crying and wiped her red, swollen eyes. "Thank God."

Bartok, Jesse, Lia and Cass waited another hour before a nurse came and took Lia into a room at the end of the hall.

When Lia was gone Cass put her head on Jesse's shoulder. "I hope he survives," she said.

"We all do," Bartok said.

After ten minutes Lia returned. When she joined her friends she burst into tears again. "He's really hurt bad. She almost killed him."

"What did they say about his chances?" Cass asked.

"He has a good chance of surviving," Lia said between sobs.

Cass put her arms around Lia and tried to comfort her. "Try to stop crying. You'll make yourself sick."

"How long will he have to be in the hospital?" Bartok asked.

"A while," Lia said.

"Let's go back to the boat," Jesse said.

They all went outside and caught a cab pulling out of the parking lot of the hospital. The driver dropped them at Gate Six.

At the entrance to the Van Damme boat at the gangplank a policeman was stationed. When Lia and Cass tried to go up, they were stopped.

"Sorry you can't have access to the boat. It's a crime scene," he said.

"Where are we supposed to stay?" asked Lia.

"I don't know, but not here," the policeman answered.

"Can I get some of my clothes?" she asked.

"Not today. Maybe tomorrow," he said.

Cass was thinking of all the dope on board. If Howard survived he would probably be arrested.

"What should we do?" Cass asked turning to Lia.

"We can get a room in town until we can get back on the boat," Lia said.

"You girls can stay on my boat tonight and then decide what you want to do tomorrow," Jesse offered.

The girls looked at each other and agreed. "Thanks, Jesse," Cass said. She squeezed his arm.

"I'm headed for my boat," Bartok said. "If you ladies need anything don't hesitate to come and ask." He waved and headed down the pier.

"Let's go to the Kettle Deli and get a pizza and take it on board. We'll want something to eat later," Jesse suggested.

"What will happen to all the dope on the Van Damme?" Lia asked.

"If the cops find it, it will be confiscated. And Howard will be arrested," Jesse said.

"Did he hide it in a good place?" Cass asked.

"Yes. Howard keeps it in the wheel house, under the wheel. Hopefully they won't think to look there. The coke and hash are in there, there is some grass in the coffee house, but very little."

The three of them headed for the Kettle Deli to order a pizza.

10

George and Etta Powers toured with the Winter Brother's Circus for twenty five years. They traveled all over the United States and performed several shows in Hawaii and Alaska. Their only son, Jesse left the family several years ago, no longer wanting to perform the trapeze act that his parents had put together. The reason he gave was that his sister, Claire fell from the high wire while doing a difficult feat and was paralyzed from the waist down. He told his parents it was their fault for insisting she do the feat. George and Etta felt bad but denied it was their fault. They insisted Claire wanted to do the stunt. However, Jesse went his own way and hadn't been in touch with his parents for a long time. The Powers cared for their daughter as best they could while on the road traveling. She spent her days in a wheel chair.

The Powers were playing in Napa at the Fair Grounds and being in Northern California Jesse came to both of their minds.

"Wonder if we can contact Jesse," George said.

"We don't have an address or phone number. I doubt it," said Etta.

"The last time we saw him he was in Sausalito," George mused. "Maybe we could drive there and see if we run into him."

"We could, George, but we'd have to rent a car

and I don't know the way. And it's a long shot that we would run into him."

George lowered his head. "Yeah, I guess you're right."

"I could call Bartok and see if he knows where Jesse is," Etta said.

His face brightened. "Hey, that sounds like a super idea. Would you do that tonight?"

Etta nodded. "As soon as we finish the trapeze set up, I'll do it." Etta harbored her own reservations as to whether she wanted to see Jesse again.

Before Jesse left there had been an awful argument. Both she and Jesse said cruel things to each other. Though she and George denied responsibility for Claire's accident, secretly Etta did feel some blame. At the last minute, Claire had turned to her mother and said, "I don't want to climb up there. I'm not feeling sure of myself." Etta told her it would ruin the act if she didn't do her part on the trapeze. So Claire climbed the ladder and when she was supposed to swing into her father's hands, she slipped off the platform and didn't quite make the reach. She fell into the net but hit a part of the structure of the platform on the way down. It injured her spine below the waist and the doctors said she would not walk again. Etta never told anyone what Claire had said to her just before she climbed the ladder.

Etta shook her head as the memories flooded her mind. She went into their trailer and found her phone book and located Bartok's number. The phone book went into her pocket until time to call.

After overseeing the building of the structure and platform for their act in the big circus arena, she and George ate a simple supper of canned spaghetti and some canned fruit. Then she went to the phone outside the office. She dialed the last number she had for Bartok.

"Hello." Bartok's baritone came over the phone on his houseboat.

"Bartok, this is Etta Powers. How are you?"

A silence and then, "I'm fine, how are you?"

"We're good. We're in Napa for two weeks with the circus and I was wondering if you knew where Jesse was?"

"I think I know how to contact him. What do you want me to say?" Bartok sounded noncommittal.

"George and I would like to see him. Could you ask him if we could drive down and visit him?"

"I'll ask," Bartok replied.

"We'd have to rent a car but we want to see him. It's been years."

"I know," Bartok said.

There was a long silence on the phone line.

"Would you give him this number if he wants to call us? Could you call us back and let us know?"

"Okay."

Etta gave the number of the phone booth at the circus. "Thanks, Bartok."

"You're welcome." Bartok hung up.

Etta hoped that Bartok would keep his word and contact Jesse. She knew Bartok had mixed feelings about the family's problems. He often took Jesse's side in blaming Etta and George for Claire's accident. Suddenly Etta started to grieve the loss of Jesse. Tears streamed down her cheeks and she wiped them away with her sleeve. She'd just have to wait to hear back from Bartok.

11

*L*ia sat beside Howard in the hospital bed. His chest and shoulder were bandaged and he had a shunt in his arm for injecting drugs besides being hooked up to a heart monitor. She held his hand and tried to quiet her thoughts.

She had been on the fence about transferring to UC Berkeley until this happened. Now, she was thinking maybe this would be a good thing. Faye would probably go to prison, Howard would divorce her and they could have a life together. Of course there were Howard's kids to consider. Was that what she really wanted? She wasn't sure if she was in love with Howard, enough to marry him. But she certainly would live with him for a while to see if they were compatible. She could finish up school in Berkley and then decide whether to go to graduate school. She was planning on being a college professor of German so she needed a PhD for that.

Howard opened his eyes and saw Lia beside him. "Hi babe," he said softly.

She leaned down and kissed his mouth. "Hi, yourself."

"How long have I been here?"

"This is the second day."

"What happened to Faye?"

"The police arrested her and are holding her in jail."

"What about the kids?"

Lia shook her head. She hadn't even thought of them. "I don't know."

"You need to look in my address book on the boat and call Faye's apartment. See who's watching the kids. The address book is on my desk. Please do this for me?" He looked beseechingly at her.

She nodded. "They won't let us on the boat, yet."

"Go to the police station. Explain about the kids. They may be all by themselves in the apartment. They'll get the address book for you."

"What about what's under the wheel?" Lia said softly.

"If you haven't heard anything, they probably haven't found it."

"Last night they said we might be able to get our clothes off the boat today. If they let us I'll find your address book."

"Thanks honey." Howard closed his eyes and drifted immediately back to sleep.

Lia left and drove her MG back to the boat. She went to the gangplank and the yellow ribbon was down. The policeman was nearby talking to some people. When he came over to the boat Lia asked, "Can I get my clothes now?"

"Sure. The crime lab has been here and gone. You're free to move back in and clean up the mess on the boat if you want."

"Thanks," Lia said as she started up the gangplank.

She walked over to where Howard was shot and looked at the deck. Dried blood stained the wood. It would take some scrubbing to get it up.

Lia shuddered at the memory of what happened and the pain it had caused Howard.

She went to the wheel house, found the address book on his desk, wondering if Howard's two children were home alone. She lifted the wheel and underneath in a deep cubby hole the dope was still hidden.

I ought to throw it in the Bay, she thought. It's so dangerous, especially the Cocaine. But she didn't, because it wasn't hers to dispose of and she figured Howard would be very angry if he found out she had dumped thousands of dollars worth of Cocaine in the Bay. Besides it wouldn't be good for the fish.

Lia left the boat and headed down the pier to Jesse's boat. She told Cass about Howard's kids in San Francisco possibly alone in the apartment.

"Maybe we ought to call right away," Cass suggested.

"We can go over to Bartok's boat and use his telephone," Jesse said.

They all walked over to the houseboat. Bartok was on deck holding up one of his finished paintings.

"Hey," he greeted them. "Just finished this masterpiece and it's ready for drying."

Lia and Cass admired the latest work of Bartok's.

Lia told him the police were gone and the Van Damme was open. "We can go aboard and clean up and move back in," she said.

"How's Howard?" Bartok asked.

"He's doing better. Not completely out of danger yet, but the doctor thinks he will recover."

"That's good news. Jesus, that wife was a tiger. I feel for Howard," Bartok commented.

"By the way, the kids may be at Faye's apartment alone. Howard wants me to call and see what's going on," Lia said.

"Sure, go ahead." Bartok pointed toward the cabin where his phone was.

Lia and Cass went downstairs and Lia dialed the number.

"Hello."

"Hi, is this Faye Bateman's apartment?" Lia asked.

"Yes, where is she?"

"Uh...I'm calling about the children. Are they there?"

"Yes. I'm the babysitter Carol, and she was supposed to be back last night. What happened to her? Who is this?"

"This is a friend of Faye's. She got held up. Can you stay a while longer?"

"I have to leave tonight. Who's going to relieve me?"

Lia looked at Cass. Cass could hear some of the conversation over the phone. She nodded.

Lia made a quick decision. "Uh...We'll come to the city and pick up the kids this afternoon. Can you stay until we get there?"

"Okay. Faye owes me for 24 hours."

"I'll pay you when we come over. Can you give me the address?"

The babysitter gave Lia the address and hung up.

Back on deck, Cass asked, "What are we going to do with the kids, Lia?"

Lia was shaking her head. "Don't know, guess bring them on board the Van Damme. Take care of them until Howard gets back."

"That may be a long time," Bartok said. "You know how to care for kids, Lia?" He looked at her carefully.

"It can't be too hard. Just feed them, put them to bed, what do you think?" she looked at Bartok.

He laughed out loud. "Kids can be problematic. They can be easy or difficult. We'll see which of these categories Howard's kids fall into."

"Oh God," Cass said under her breath, "looks like we have our work cut out for us."

"I'm going over to pick them up now," Lia said. "I think I'll drive Howard's van because the MG isn't big enough for all of us."

"I'll come too," Cass offered. She looked at Jesse.

"I'll stay here and try to clean up the blood on the deck," Jesse said.

"Use bleach and water," Bartok said.

"Okay. We'll be back in a couple of hours," Lia said over her shoulder as she stepped off Bartok's houseboat.

Jesse gave Cass a hug and a kiss on the mouth. "Hurry back," he said.

Cass smiled back.

The girls went up the gangplank to the Van Damme to get Howard's keys to the van.

Lia backed it out to Bridgeway and hit the freeway to the city in record time.

⌐

Jesse turned to leave Bartok's houseboat but Bartok held him by the arm.

"Stay a minute, Jesse. I want to talk to you." Bartok sat down and motioned for Jesse to take a seat.

"What's up?" Jesse asked.

Your mother called yesterday and asked me to contact you. I said I would. She wants to rent a car and drive down here from the Napa Fair Grounds to visit you. The circus is in town for two weeks."

"She can't drive worth a damn," Jesse said. "Never knows where she's going. She'll get killed on the freeway."

Jesse sat in deep thought for several minutes. Bartok respecting his silence remained quiet, too.

"Maybe I'll go up there and visit them. I'd like to see Claire. Not sure how I'll feel about Mom and Dad, though."

"You won't know until you see them." Bartok said, sagely.

"I hated my mother as well as my dad for a long time for causing Claire's accident. But I think I've let go of it now."

"Good for you. Not all of us can do that; let go of hate."

"If I go, can you handle the music one evening on the Van Damme?"

"Sure. Lia and Cass and I can take care of the coffee house."

"I was thinking of asking Cass to go with me?" He looked at Bartok with a slow smile.

"That girl gettin' to you? Be careful, you often said you weren't ready to get hitched to one girl."

"That was then, this is now," Jesse said, rolling the words off his tongue. "Hey, that could be words from a song." He started humming a tune.

"Just don't break the girl's heart, Jesse. You know you have a tendency to do that."

"I hear you. I really like Cass. I want her for my girlfriend."

Bartok nodded. "Just be tender with her. She seems pretty fragile."

"I will, Bartok." He turned to leave. "I'm off to clean up the Van Damme deck."

"Want some help?" Bartok asked.

"Sure."

"I've got some bleach on board and a pail. I think there's a mop on the Van Damme."

The two of them headed down the pier with a pail and bleach in hand.

12

$\mathcal{L}$ia turned onto Market Street and watched for Valencia. She turned right and went a couple of blocks to the correct address. Finding a parking place wasn't easy but there was an old church across the street. She pulled into the parking lot and they headed for the apartment house. Lia rang the bell for # 221. The outer door opened and the girls went up the steps to the second floor. Down the hall they could see a young girl standing outside the apartment door.

"Are you Lia?" she asked.

"Right," Lia said. "This is my friend, Cass."

Carol the babysitter took them inside to the apartment. The two children were eating at the table. Howie had his father's eyes, and dusky skin and Nancy had her mother's lovely dark hair and big dark eyes. They were eating peanut butter and jelly sandwiches.

"This is Howie and Nancy. Howie is four and Nancy is three. They cried last night because their mother wasn't here. I didn't know what happened to her. Where is she?"

Cass took Carol aside. "Faye shot her husband and has been arrested." she said quietly. "Howard is in the hospital recovering. We think he'll be all right."

"Oh my God!" Carol put her hands to her face. Then she recovered and looked at the children.

"We're going to take the kids to Sausalito on the boat where Howard has been living," continued

Cass. "We'll take care of them until he gets out of the hospital."

Carol shook her head. "I knew something was wrong when she left. She looked like she was in a trance."

She tousled Nancy's hair. "Say hi to these nice ladies. They are taking you for a ride and a visit on a boat."

Howie said "hi." Nancy said nothing, just looked at the girls with her big eyes.

"Well, good luck," Carol said to the girls. "I hope you know about small children. They demand attention. Faye owes me $25. That was our agreement if I ever did an over-nighter."

Lia took the money from her wallet and gave it to Carol. "Thanks for staying. We were afraid the kids were alone," Lia said.

"Faye is pretty flaky but I've never known her to leave the kids alone and I wouldn't either." Carol picked up her jacket. "What will happen to her?"

"We don't know yet," Lia said. "She has been arrested and is in jail. We can let you know when we find out."

Carol took out her pen and scribbled her phone number on a piece of paper on the table. "Call me at this number. Thanks. I live downstairs in this building."

"Will do," Lia said, pocketing the number.

Carol left and the girls turned to Howie and Nancy. Howie was cramming the last of his sandwich into his mouth. Nancy was eating a carrot stick.

"Hi kids. I'm Lia and this is Cass. Your mother asked us to pick you up and take you to a boat across the bridge. Doesn't that sound like fun?"

Howie shook his head. "I want Momma," he said.

"She got held up, but you'll see her soon," Lia soothed.

"Is that good to lie?" Cass said in a soft voice.

"Probably not but I thought it would calm him."

The children both finished their lunches with no more questions. Cass went into their bedroom and found some clothes which she packed in a cloth satchel. She and Lia found jackets and ushered the kids out of the apartment and down to the van.

⤺

Howard opened his eyes and took in all the hospital equipment hooked up to his body. He seemed to be breathing all right. They weren't giving him oxygen so he figured he'd live. He vaguely remembered what happened. And he remembered Lia coming to the hospital. God, he didn't want to lose her, and he knew he hadn't handled the situation between Faye and Lia well. He'd never been good at having two relationships at the same time. He always fucked it up somehow.

He didn't want to hurt Faye but he'd told her several times they were finished romantically. She just wouldn't accept it. Now when he had a chance with a real woman that he cared about, Faye took it in her mind to be jealous! Christ! What did he have to do to get Faye off his back?

Maybe this would do it. She had fucked up this time. She may have to spend time in jail. She had committed a crime and the courts would punish her for it.

Lia had come by again and said the kids were on the boat and she and Cass were taking care of them. She told him she was keeping them away from the late night parties and all the dope. They were sleeping in the room that the Cohens had occupied and they locked them in while the music was happening. They chose the room because it was right next to the Coffee House and they could check on them regularly. Lia had also moved a cot into the room and was sleeping with the children. Howie and Nancy woke up at 8 a.m. and Lia usually got to bed at 4 a.m. so she wasn't getting much sleep. She took a nap in the afternoon and Cass took over with the kids.

He'd never expected Lia to take charge of his children, but he was happy that she did. The doctor said he could go home next week sometime. Then he'd be on the boat to relieve the girls.

Funny how things worked out. The detective from the Sausalito Police Department came by to tell him they were charging Faye with attempted murder. No one had come forward to bail her out and she was still in jail after two weeks.

A young, pretty nurse came bustling into his room. "Hi Howard. We have your afternoon medicine." She had a cup of water and a small pill cup with two pills.

"Can't you find me a joint to smoke? That is better medicine than these pills." Howard pushed her hand away from his mouth but the pill cup made its way back to his mouth.

"Open wide," she said.

He knew it was no use arguing with her. He took the pills with a swig of water.

"Now be a good patient and eat your dinner," she added as she left the room. The food server came into his room and put a plate on his tray. She rolled up his bed and smiled.

He did eat half of what was on the plate; a little cut-up chicken, green beans and coleslaw. He drank his juice and thought he felt strength flowing back into his body. He didn't like being vulnerable and waited on. He must get his health back as soon as possible.

13

*J*esse rolled over in the bed and cuddled next to Cass. He could feel the gentle rocking of the bay against The Kayak. She moved away from him in her sleep. Carefully he placed his arm around her chest and fondled her breast. Her eyes flew open and she rolled over to see him staring at her.

"Good morning," she said.

"Good morning, Princess."

Cass stretched her arms above her head. "I was having this great dream. I was floating on a cloud and a lovely rainbow came and rested right beside me."

"It's always nice to have rainbows with your clouds." Jesse chuckled. He took her hand in his. "Would you like to go with me to meet my parents in Napa?"

"What? I thought you didn't stay in touch with them?"

"I don't, but they sent word through Bartok that their circus was performing at the Napa County Fair Grounds and wanted to see me."

Cass's eyes grew large. "So you are going?"

"Yup. And I'd like you to come, too."

Cass started to laugh.

"What's funny?" Jesse looked hurt.

"Nothing really. I didn't know we were at the stage of meeting parents."

"It's not that kind of thing, Cass. I'm going and I thought you'd like to ride up there with me. If you don't want to, fine. I'll go alone."

"Yes, I'd like to go with you," Cass said quickly.

Jesse leaned over and kissed her. "I'm glad. You may not like my parents but it's not important. What's important is how we feel about each other."

Cass was surprised at his assumptions. He'd never professed any love for her or special relationship. But in his mind, that's what they were in; a special relationship.

Did she want to get into a close personal relationship so soon after the divorce? She thought she didn't, but was now wavering. Was it because Jesse showed more than a little interest in her? She hoped she wasn't that starved for love and attention. She wanted to go slow but in Jesse's mind they were already a couple.

She'd meet his parents. Sometimes parents showed clues as to who their children were. She admitted Jesse was a fabulous musician and a nice dude, but he possessed no sense of loyalty or monogamy. She didn't know if she could stay in a relationship if he continued to have girls on the side. Probably the best thing was for her to wait to see what developed between them.

She dressed more carefully than usual. Picking out a pair of blue peddle-pushers with matching top and sandals, she hoped this looked more presentable than her granny dresses.

⌐

Jesse borrowed Howard's VW bus with the tie-dye curtains. The drive up north was lovely; Cass hadn't seen the hills of Marin, now a golden brown, and Jesse made a detour to Petaluma, a small town on the way that catered to the hippie crowd. They stopped at a Health Food Market that had a little café inside and ordered coffee and lunch. The locals could have been from Venice down south, or Berkeley in the East Bay, the way they were dressed in tie-dye clothing and bell bottoms. A guitar player and a mandolin player were sitting outside the market playing and drew quite a crowd.

Jesse drove on to Napa to the Fair Grounds. They pulled into the parking lot. Cass could see all kinds of rides, ferris wheels, merry-go-rounds, games that gave away prizes for the best shots, a fat lady and the skinniest man alive.

It wasn't difficult to spot the Big Tent where Jesse's parents did their trapeze act. He entered the tent and saw his father standing beside one of the ladders.

When he turned and saw Jesse he froze in place for a moment. Then he called, "Jesse, my son. How wonderful to see you."

Jesse and Cass walked over to his father. "Dad," Jesse said as he put out his hand. His father chose to ignore it and pulled him to his chest.

"I'm so glad you made the trip up here." He looked at Cass. "Who do we have here?"

"This is Cass, my old lady," Jesse said.

George gave Cass a smile. "So you've corralled my son. Good for you."

"Nice to meet you Mr. Powers," Cass said.

"George, please. Come, let's find your mother." George turned toward the back of the tent with his arm around Jesse's shoulders.

George was dressed in overhauls, sweatshirt, and a headband on his head to hold back his longish hair. He was tall, strong and quite well built.

Ahead, Cass saw a tiny woman in a long skirt with long gray hair wound into a bun. She was dressed much like the hippies in Sausalito.

When she saw her son, she ran to him. "Jesse," she said, embracing him and kissing him on the cheek. When she stepped back she looked from Jesse to George to Cass.

"Mother, this is Cass, my old lady," Jesse explained for a second time. "Cass, this is Etta."

Etta's eyes took in the long dark hair and dark eyes. "Hello Cass."

Cass was just recovering from being introduced as his 'old lady' twice. She got her wits about her and greeted Etta. "Hello Mrs. Powers."

"Etta," she said.

Jesse looked around. "Where is Claire?"

"She's probably in our trailer. Let's go and get her," Etta said.

They all walked out of the back of the tent to a large trailer. Etta opened the door and called, "Claire, come see who's here?"

Shortly a wheel chair appeared at the doorway and the small, beautiful girl in it saw Jesse. "Oh my Lord," she exclaimed. "Jesse." She held out her arms and he was in them before anyone could blink.

He gave her a tight hug and she kissed him on the cheek.

"Let's go inside and sit a spell," Etta said.

Claire moved her chair out of the way and the four moved inside. Cass could see the trailer was fairly large; a big living room, a good sized kitchen and eating area.

Jesse's sister, Claire, was a lovely small girl with dark hair and eyes. Her legs were hidden under a shawl.

Etta offered tea or coffee and everyone declined.

"Where are you living, now," George asked.

In Sausalito," Jesse replied.

"Care to give us your mailing address?"

"I'm living on a boat, Dad. It's not a permanent address and I have no mail drop."

Jesse's dad was silent.

"Are you still playing guitar and singing," asked Claire.

"Yes. I'm in the process of forming a band. We hope to get some gigs around the Bay Area."

Etta was busy in the kitchen. She brought two plates of pie, handing one to Jesse and the other to Cass. "I baked this yesterday," she said to her son. "I didn't know you were coming, but I know how you love apple pie."

"Aren't you going to have some, Dad and Claire?"

"We already had pie for lunch," Claire said with a smile.

"Uh…you still doing the same high-wire act?" Jesse addressed his Dad.

"Yup. Except it's only the two of us now since Claire uh…had her accident."

"Have you been to the doctor lately, Claire? Any chance you can walk again?"

She shook her head and looked away. "No. The doctor who examined me right after the accident said my spine was injured so badly I couldn't support my legs." The shawl had slipped slightly and Cass could see, below her brown peddle-pushers, Claire's thin legs. She looked away quickly.

"Now Jesse, don't be bringing up unhappy subjects," George said. "We try to keep Claire's mind off from those things."

"What, are you in denial, Dad? Have such a guilty conscious that you can't talk about it?"

"Now Jesse, don't fight with your Dad," Etta chimed in. "He only means well for Claire."

"Yeah, sure." Jesse finished his pie and laid his plate on the side table. "We got to be going."

"Oh Jesse, stay a little longer, please," Claire begged.

Cass put her hand on Jesse's arm and he sat back down. "Ok, for a little while."

Etta went to the desk and pulled out a photo album. "Here are some of the pictures we have taken over the years." She handed it to Jesse.

Jesse took it and he sat on a chair beside Claire's wheelchair and they looked through the album.

"How do you know our son," George asked Cass.
I uh…met him through his music," she said.

"Are you a musician, too?" Etta asked.

Cass shook her head. "No, I'm a listener."

"She has a lovely voice," Jesse spoke up. "She can sing like a songbird."

Cass was sure she was blushing. "Not really. I mostly sing folk music."

"We'd love to come to one of your concerts, Jesse," Claire said. "Would you let us know when and where?"

"Claire you know we aren't going to be here beyond two weeks," her father said. "That's the circus's run here."

She looked down. "I know. Where are we going next? Maybe we could come back for one of his concerts?"

Her mother shook her head. "We're headed for Washington, Bellingham, next stop for the circus."

"Jesse squeezed his sister's hand. "Don't worry. If I ever get famous, I'll bring you back to the Bay Area for a gig. Okay?"

Claire nodded and put her arm around his shoulders.

Jesse stood. "Now we do have to go. We have some errands to do yet."

"Thanks for coming, son," Etta said. She walked over and hugged him and kissed him on the cheek. Jesse embraced his mother, leaned down and hugged Claire again. There were tears in her eyes. He walked over to his Dad and offered his hand. This time his father took it.

He and Cass left quickly, not looking back. "Let's get out of here, pronto," Jesse said quietly.

When they got to the VW van, Jesse slid in the driver's side and started the motor, skidding out of the parking lot.

"Are you okay?" Cass asked.

"Yeah."

"I'm glad you brought me with you. I liked meeting your parents and Claire."

"They ruined her life. She'll always be tied to the wheelchair. Who's going to marry her? And she can't have children. What kind of life is that? To have to travel with a circus you can't perform in."

Cass was silent. She had no answers for Jesse.

14

$\mathcal{L}$ia fixed dinner for Howie and Nancy. The children were sitting at one of the picnic tables in The Ark. Howie was playing with his spaghetti and Nancy was trying to swallow a peanut butter sandwich.

Jesse and Cass came into the coffee house after returning from Napa.

"Did everything go all right?" Lia asked.

"If you mean did we get into a fight, no," Jesse said.

"How's it going here?" Cass asked.

"Okay. I took the kids to the hospital today and they saw their Dad." Lia spoke softly so the kids couldn't hear. "He told them he had a car accident."

"Is no one going to tell them where Faye is?" Cass asked softly.

"I don't think so, I'm certainly not. They're only three and four, Cass." She looked crossly at her friend.

"When is Howard getting out of the hospital," Jesse asked.

"In a few days, the doctor says."

"What's happening with F.?" He asked.

"No one knows. Howard doesn't and I don't," Lia said.

The children finished eating and were getting restless. "I wanna play," Nancy said.

"What do you want to play?" Lia asked.

"Paper dolls," she said.

"Go get your paper dolls and we'll play," Lia said. She winked at Cass. "Looks like I'm getting training for a role later in life."

Nancy hopped off the bench and raced down the deck to the room the kids were sharing.

"What are you two up too?" Lia asked.

"I have some guys coming over to my boat later and we're practicing some of my songs. I plan on putting a band together."

"Who will be in it," Lia asked.

"John on keyboard and Dave on bass guitar and I'll do 12-string guitar and vocals. We're going to call ourselves Desperados. "

This was the first Cass had heard of this. "Hey, you didn't tell me, that's great!"

"The guys that I usually play with here at The Ark, I figured they'd want to form a band. I ran it by them the other day and they all seemed excited about it. I already have this song in my head, *Napa County Circus Blues*. I gotta go write it down." He turned to Cass. "Come on over and sit in or listen when you feel like it." He waved to Lia and left.

Lia gave Cass a serious look. "Looks like you'll be busy for awhile."

Nancy came back with the box of paper dolls and Lia spread them on the table.

"I want to play ball," Howie said.

"Why don't I take him over to Jesse's boat for a while and let him listen to some fine music?"

"What if the guys are smokin'?"

"So what? It's not going to hurt him. He won't know it's any different from cigarettes."

Lia quickly agreed. "It would help me. I've had my hands full figuring out what to do to please both of them at the same time."

Cass leaned down toward his face. "How about we go listen to some dudes play some good music on another boat, Howie?"

"Another boat? Okay." Howie loved boats.

Lia watched Cass and Howie walked down the gangplank toward Jesse's boat. Howie waved his little hand at Lia. She waved back.

The guitars tuning up could be heard all the way to the Van Damme. Kayak greeted them on deck. Cass lifted Howie onto the boat and they went down the steps to the cabin. David, Spence, John and Jesse were seated around the cabin. Spence had set up a small drum set. Jesse pointed Cass to the table and chairs there. She swung Howie up into a chair and sat beside the child.

"We are going to sit quietly and listen to the music, okay? We aren't going to talk because that would disturb the musicians."

Howie's eyes were round as he nodded his agreement.

"Let's play that song I recently taught you, *Together Again*, Jesse said to the band, passing a joint. Spence took a toke passed it on. They began playing and Jesse turned up the volume. His 12-string nearly drowned out the other guitars.

John Leggovinia was an old friend of Jesse's and played keyboard. They had gotten each other out of jams numerous times. John was quiet, usually had good judgment and rarely enjoyed a girl friend. He was tall, gangly, dark haired with Mediterranean skin.

Spence Draper was a musician friend; he and Jesse had played in numerous groups together but never for money. He was a terrific drummer, kind of played to his own beat and the others matched his rhythms. Short, dark with an outgoing personality, he got along with most everyone.

David Caplan was another story. He was a ladies' man, love them and leave them type, great guitarist, often played with several outstanding bands around the Bay Area, including Jerry Garcia's group. Cute and sexy, he had an outgoing personality, too.

Howie grinned broadly and wiggled around in his seat to the music. Cass was happy to be a listener.

When they came to a stop, Jesse said, "Cass, sing along with me." He handed her a paper with the words on it.

She took it and when the music started again she tried to match the words to the music Jesse was singing, but it was difficult. They practiced the song several more times and then took a beer break.

Howie's eyes were drooping, so Cass laid him on the floor on a blanket under the table. She didn't want anyone to stumble over him.

After the break, the band went back to some serious practicing. Cass moved up by Jesse and could hear him singing the melody better and was able to sing along. A few hours later they stopped. David and Spence had to leave.

"Tomorrow afternoon, practice," said Jesse. The guys all agreed.

"What are we calling our band?" John said.

"I thought Desperados...what do you think?"Jesse had already decided but thought he'd better check in with the guys.

They looked at each other and nodded. "Sounds like a good name," Spence said.

Back on the Van Damme, Cass helped Lia make some dinner for the kids and the rest of the crowd that was hanging around. Howard usually barbecued burgers or hot dogs and the girls made potato salad or a bean salad. There was always bread, buns and two or three variety of chips. Lia had picked up some vegetables for a salad for the kids, tomatoes, cucumbers and lettuce.

"Aren't we giving the kids some healthy food," joked Cass.

"Yes, I don't want them to get sick on my watch."

"I wouldn't want them to get sick at all. Looks like you're taking good care of them. I can give Howard a good report," Cass said with a smile.

"Did that joker ask you to report to him what I fed the kids?" Lia demanded.

"Nawww...just kidding you."

"How'd the practice go?"

"Pretty good. Those guys are good. Jesse had me singing along with him."

"Bet he's planning on you being in the band," Lia said.

"I don't think so. I can't sing well enough," Cass denied.

"Cass O'Brien, you sing as well as Joanie. What are you talking about?"

"Thanks for your support, Lia, but no, I can't compare to Joan Baez. I do try, though."

By the way, I wanted to hear how it went with Jesse's parents up in Napa?"

Cass threw her a somber look. "There's serious anger between Jesse and his father. I think he loves his sister a lot and was terribly upset when she had the accident. He blames his parents."

"How is the sister doing?"

"Claire is a lovely girl, but can't use her legs to walk. I don't think she has much of a life traveling around with a circus she can't participate in."

"That's sad," Lia said as she finished the potato salad. "Do you think Jesse would grill the hot dogs I bought for the crowd?"

"Probably. We'll ask him when he comes over."

I'm just going to boil the kids hot dogs. I need to feed them on schedule. They get hungry a lot and are cranky if they have to wait."

Cass told Lia how good Howie was and fell asleep listening to the music.

"Amazing he could sleep with all the guitars and drums blaring. I could hear them over here."

"Children are resilient and flexible," Cass said.

"Let's hope they are toward their mother when she shows up again in their lives."

The girls prepared the dinner for the people staying on the boat and the musicians who played every night. When Jesse arrived, Lia asked him to take over the barbecuing and he agreed. Soon people and musicians filtered back onto the boat and began eating the evening meal.

15

$\mathcal{H}$oward's stay in the hospital was three weeks. Things were going fairly well on the Van Damme. Lia and Cass tried to keep things together. Every night the musicians came and there was food to prepare. Bartok brought food and helped with the evening's entertainment as did Jesse. The boat no longer provided the drugs as Howard wasn't there, so the musicians and guests brought their own weed and Cocaine. Lia asked everyone to leave Heroin off the boat because of the presence of the children and everyone agreed.

Nancy and Howie became used to the comings and goings of people on the Van Damme and seemed to settle into the life they were leading. Lia and Cass doted on them, not letting them out of their sight.

Howard was coming home today and everyone was excited. The children hadn't asked about Faye, their mother except for one time, when they first came on the boat. Lia and Cass had kept the kids attention with unusual things to do. Now they were happy that their Dad would be back with them.

Lia left with Bartok to pick up Howard. Cass and Jesse prepared a feast for all who would be there that evening; Jesse grilling chicken and zucchini strips, Cass made a large bean salad and a green tomato salad. She and Lia had baked three carrot cakes and frosted them. Lia changed the bedding in the wheel house, but Bartok and Jesse had brought a single mattress up from below deck and laid it on deck near the picnic table. Lia and Cass made it up with clean sheets and a blanket. Several pillows were thrown on for Howard to prop himself up.

When Howard arrived in his VW van with Bartok driving, a group of people on the dock came over to welcome him home. Nearly all of the houseboat community was there.

Bartok and Jesse helped him up the gangplank, supporting his arms as he still didn't have his strength back. They walked him to the mattress on deck and gently lowered him to the bed.

Lia, on her knees, gave him a big hug and kiss. "Welcome home, babe." She said.

Cass kissed his cheek and ruffled his hair. "Needs combing," she said playfully.

"Are you hungry, want something to drink?" Lia asked.

"First I want to smoke a joint. I think I must have gone cold turkey while in the hospital. I feel clean as a new born babe."

Jesse pulled a joint out of his pocket and lit it up, handing it to Howard. Suddenly Howie and Nancy came running out of their room. "Daddy, Daddy," they shouted.

Before anyone could stop them they both threw themselves at the mattress. Nancy landed on his legs, but Howie ended up on Howard's chest. "Oww...careful son, Daddy's still hurting."

Lia grabbed Howie and sat him down beside his Dad. Nancy was crawling up his legs toward his chest. Lia pulled her down and sat her beside Howie.

"Your daddy is still injured. You have to be careful of him," she explained to the children.

Both of the kids took turns hugging Howard around the neck with Lia carefully supervising.

The children jabbered with their Dad for a few minutes, and then Lia brought a glass of water.

"You need to drink this," she said.

"What's this?" Howard asked as he took another hit from the joint.

"The doctor said you must drink a lot of water every day. Less Scotch and more water. I'm just making sure you follow orders."

Howard laughed and then winced at a pain in his shoulder.

"Okay, I guess I have to follow orders. But he didn't say I couldn't have all the dope I want."

"I didn't ask him, but I suspect he would say grass is *all* that's okay," Lia commented.

"In honor of returning home, we need to light a bong," Jesse said, as he began preparing it.

Everyone started getting high. People began pouring in for the evening's entertainment.

Cass took the kids to their room and stayed with them until they fell asleep. When she left the room she locked the door.

The food was brought out and the Scotch and Vodka

were opened. Lots of illegal substances and food began showing up. Howard's bed was moved into The Ark coffeehouse and the music began. The party was on...

⌒

It was a beautiful, sunny day in the boat community of Gate Six. The cloudless sky glowed powder blue; the ships sparkled like cut glass in the sun. The sea shone like a glossy, smooth carpet. The sea gulls and cormorants glided across the water. Cass, Jesse, Howard and Lia lay sprawled on the deck chairs taking in the sun. Nancy and Howie colored at the table. Kayak rested beside the table.

Two men dressed in suits, ties and fedoras walked up the gangplank. Cass guessed they came from the Sausalito Police Department.

"Howard Bateman?" one of them said.

Howard held up his hand and struggled up. "Yes, can I help you?"

"I'm Detective Moran and this is Detective Allen. We wanted to let you know that your wife, Faye Bateman's arraignment is coming up on Monday and you are needed in court," Moran said.

"Of course, I'll be there. What time?"

"9 a.m."

"Thanks, guys," Howard said. "Do I need to do anything or bring anything with me?"

"At that time, the judge will consider custody of the children. If you ask the court for custody you'll probably get it. Your wife is going to be given a psychiatric examination."

Howard nodded. "Do you think she will get hard time?"

"I can't answer that, but she seems disturbed. She will most likely be sent to a psychiatric facility, but I can't promise."

"Thanks."

The two detectives looked at the children coloring, one of them smiled and they left the Van Damme.

"Jesus, Faye will be in a shrink ward," Howard murmured.

"That might be the best place for her right now," Lia said.

"I'll have to go over and dismantle her apartment and get rid of the stuff in it. Bring the kids toys and stuff over here." Howard was thinking out loud.

"We'll help," Lia said. "You're not well enough yet."

"In another two weeks I'll be strong enough and that's the end of the month. I'll contact her landlord so he doesn't get rid of anything."

"We'll all help," Jesse said.

"Me too," Bartok chimed in.

Cass and Lia exchanged glances that said, never a dull minute around here.

⌐

Howard showed up on crutches for Faye's arraignment accompanied by Lia and Bartok. Cass and Jesse stayed on the boat to take care of Howie and Nancy.

The Judge asked if any of Faye's family were there and was informed her parents were both deceased.

Faye looked at Howard and cried buckets of tears, but he was unmoved. He testified under oath on the stand that she shot him twice. Based on the psychiatric evaluation the judge sent Faye to Napa State Hospital and full custody of the children was given to Howard.

Now he had two extra responsibilities and he felt unqualified to take care of the children. Thank God he had Lia and Cass to help.

That evening everyone in the houseboat community came on board the Van Damme for the party. They were celebrating the addition of Nancy and Howie to the community. The crowd cut back their coke usage dramatically, not doing it in front of the children, and no Heroin on board. Cass thought she would never see anything that selfless from the boat people.

However, the joints kept on rolling out, and everyone got stoned. The music began and Nancy and Howie were allowed to fall asleep listening. Lia and Cass carried them to bed in the room on deck.

Cass sang with Jesse and his newly formed band. She was learning Jesse's songs and she did lend a nice balance to the group with her lilting soprano weaving around the minor notes.

Around 3 a.m. Cass told Jesse she was going to bed. He'd said he'd be down later.

When he climbed in next to Cass it was 5 a.m. "What took you so long?" she said sleepily.

"Oh, I had to fight off a couple of groupie girls that wanted a threesome."

Cass came wide-awake. "Really?"

"Naw, just joshing you."

"Has everyone left?" she asked.

"Just about. Howard and Lia are going to sleep in the room with the kids tonight."

"They aren't getting much together time," Cass murmured, snuggling down next to Jesse.

"I'm sure they'll make up for it, later. Right now, Howard's not all that well, and he didn't want the kids waking up without anyone in the room."

"I don't think Lia knew what she was getting into when she made this trip up here."

"Neither did you," he said.

16

Cass and Jesse worked on his boat with the band, practicing. A young girl came on board, tramping down the steps to the cabin and stood in the doorway. She was about fifteen, looked like a runaway as she was very dirty and her clothes were soiled. She also looked stoned.

"Jesse?" she asked.

"Who's asking," Jesse said.

"I'm Gretchen. I was here a few weeks ago. Thought I'd visit you."

"We're pretty busy right now, practicing. I'm sorry I don't have time to visit."

The girl looked devastated. "But, I thought I could get high and stay for a while."

"Sorry, not possible." Jesse looked at Cass for help. "No way," she said to him, shaking her head.

He got up from his stool, ushered the girl up on deck and off the boat.

"Now if you come back, I'll have to call the police. I don't want you on the boat anymore."

She turned to go and had tears in her eyes as she left.

Jesse went down into the cabin. He glanced over at Cass who was avoiding his eyes.

He went over to her and leaned down. "She happened before I met you, honey. I'm sorry."

Cass pushed Jesse's head out of her space. "Okay. Go back and practice," she said, and after a few more songs she left.

⤸

Jesse bounded up the gangplank of The Ark. "I've got us a paying gig, this Saturday at the No Name Bar downtown," he shouted to Cass, Lia and Howard who were on deck smoking a joint.

"Bitchin'," Howard said.

"Cool," Lia and Cass chimed in.

"And you are going to be our songbird." Jesse pointed at Cass.

"Uh...no, Jesse. I'm not ready."

"Of course you are. Ready as you'll ever by. Don't worry sweetheart. I'll carry you along if you forget the words."

Lia clapped her hands. "Far-out, Cass. You'll be singing with a real live band for money."

Cass didn't look at all happy. Her long face turned toward her friends. "I don't know if I can sing before an audience."

"It's no different than singing here on the boat," Lia said.

"That's true, honey," Jesse agreed. "We'll smoke a joint before we go on and everything will flow..."

Cass wasn't sure she would be able to do a whole show.

"I'll have all the words printed out for you and if you get in a jam, I'll hand them to you and you can read them. I have to go over to Bartok's and call the guys and tell them. Be right back."

Jesse ran down the gangplank and down the dock to the Valley-Ho.

"He is so excited," Cass said smiling.

"It's great that he got a gig so quickly," Howard said. "Jesse's songs and his reputation as a musician are pretty well-known around Sausalito. The No Name Bar likes local groups, so it's not too surprising."

Cass had a lump in her throat. She was still trying to get used to singing with the band.

⌒

Saturday night came more swiftly than Cass had expected. The band practiced five hours a day and was in good shape for their virgin paying gig.

In the dressing room, just before they took the stage, Jesse called Cass over and pointed to a line of coke.

She shook her head. "I think I'll stay straight the first time."

"Okay, babe, hang loose." Jesse leaned down and did a line. Each of the band members snorted a line, and then they all went on stage to setup their instruments.

There were maybe forty people in the audience, an assortment of bar people, some in booths and some at tables. Lia and Howard, who was getting around fairly well on a pair of crutches, were there as well.

The California sound was in the process of a metamorphosis. The folk music sounds of Simon and Garfunkel,

Joan Baez and Bob Dylan, enhanced by the Beach Boys sound and the rhythm and blues influence, along with jazz had blended into a composition of new sounds with the addition of rockabilly. Bands were experimenting with new notes and improvisations. What was born out of this happy sound would soon be called, folk-rock.

Jesse was writing songs in the genre of folk-rock. The Desperados still played *Together Again*, the song Jesse sold to Paul Zanes, the record producer. The song hadn't been released yet on the new album. Tonight they would introduce two of Jesse's latest songs, *Napa County Circus Blues*, and *Only Love*. Cass had learned the words and she felt half-way confident she could sing them all the way through.

Jesse, David and Spence tuned up and began the evening's music. Cass took the mike and the blending of their voices and instruments pleased the audience.

After an hour, the band took a break. Drinks were comped to the band but Cass passed on the alcohol.

Howard and Lia came back stage and congratulated the group on a nice first set.

"Thanks," Jesse said. He was smiling broadly and very happy.

Cass was also happy… happy that she'd not forgotten the words, only had to read them a couple of times and had kept the harmony going with Jesse.

Before the band returned to the stage, Paul Zanes came back stage. "I heard a couple of new compositions, Jesse. Want to sell them?"

"Uh...I have to talk it over with Cass, first," Jesse said.

Paul eyed Cass. "Okay. I'll give you a good deal on both of the new ones."

"We'll get in touch later, Paul," Cass said.

Paul was hesitant to leave it at that. "When can we get together?"

"We'll call you," Cass said.

Jesse hurried the band out to the stage and they left Paul standing there.

The second set went nearly as well as the first. Cass was tiring and her voice became a little ragged at times. She wasn't used to singing full tilt for an hour at a time. This was the second hour.

After the applause, the band went back stage and lit a joint. Cass could see Paul making his way backstage from the audience.

Cass saw Lia and Howard also on their way backstage. They intercepted Paul. Whatever Howard said, Paul turned around and left the No Name Bar.

When Lia and Howard came up the steps backstage, Cass asked, "What did you say to Paul?"

"I told him to stop harassing Jesse. That he would be calling him when he was ready."

"Thanks, friend," Jesse said. He slapped Howard lightly on his undamaged shoulder. "I'm going to let Cass take care of it. She seems to be good at it."

Cass was beaming. "My new calling...negotiating contracts for musicians."

"Just me, babe," Jesse said possessively. "And you're my new songbird with the band."

"I'd like the four of us to sit down later and seriously talk about what would be fair and negotiable for Jesse's songs," Cass proposed. "Would you two help us?" She looked at Howard and Lia.

"Sounds like a good idea," Howard said.

After midnight the band packed up and left the No Name Bar and headed back to The Ark where local singers and musicians had taken over for the night. Bartok had overseen the food and drugs and watched over Nancy and Howie after Lia and Howard had put them to bed. When The Desperados arrived, Jim, one of the regulars on the boat was playing and singing. The band joined him and began jamming.

Cass, Lia and Howard had a late supper after Lia checked on the kids.

"Not a peep out of them," Bartok assured Howard. "They were tired puppies after fishing all afternoon."

"Did they catch anything?" Cass asked, having been on Jesse's boat practicing all afternoon.

Bartok shook his head. "Not really. I helped them pull in a couple of fish just so they could scream with excitement."

"You are a good godfather, Bartok," Lia said, kissing the top of his head.

Cass left the music and crept downstairs to her bed around 3 a.m. Jesse was still jamming upstairs.

17

Faye lifted her head from the pillow. She felt her mind trying to come out of the mist. There were bars on the windows, white walls, her white bed covers, and her green gown. She looked out the barred window. Trees blew in the wind, birds glided from one tree to another and the sun was shining.

Where was she? What had happened? She knew in the cloud of her mind that something terribly important had taken place but she couldn't figure out what.

She stepped out of bed. Her bare feet touched the cold tiles of the floor and chilled her. Noticing a book on the table, she picked it up. Napa County Hospital was written across the top. The title read, *Suggestions for Patients During their Incarceration.*

My God! She was in a hospital. She must have had a breakdown! She couldn't remember anything. Only that she thought she had two children...somewhere. What were their names? She searched her mind, still foggy. Yes, Nancy, and Howie. Where were they? How had she arrived in this barren place?

She ran to the door that had a small window in the top. "Help me...Help me...please," She cried out. Tears ran down her face and she sobbed as she walked back and threw herself on the bed.

⌐

The Desperados were making a name for themselves in Sausalito. So far, Jesse had not tried for a gig in San Francisco, content to play for locals. The band was paid $25 a night so that meant each band member received $5.00. Not very much, but Jesse said this was just the beginning.

Every time they played, dozens of young groupies ran on stage after the show and mobbed the musicians, hugging them and trying to kiss them. Jesse was particularly targeted as he was handsome and the lead singer along with Cass. Cass was getting sick of the entire scene.

One Saturday morning, she approached Jesse at the breakfast table in The Ark galley.

"I want you to hire a bouncer or someone who will keep the young girls away. I'm not going to be humiliated anymore."

"Babe, they don't know you're my old lady. They don't mean any disrespect. They are just reacting to the music."

"I don't care. I'm not singing anymore with the band unless you do something about this."

Cass stood up and stalked off.

Jesse sat in thought over his eggs and bacon. Maybe the guys would know someone who they could hire for a few bucks a night. He'd give up his share of the gig's money, to pay someone. They were getting double what they had started being paid. And he could use some of the money Paul had paid him for the song, "Together Again."

The four of them had sat down later that morning and tried to come to a consensus as to how much to charge for Jesse's songs.

"I think $300 is a good amount. That's what Paul paid for the first song," Jesse suggested.

Howard, Lia and Cass were of the opinion to ask a lot more. The band was beginning to be known in Sausalito. "I think Jesse should ask at least $500 per song," Howard said.

"Yes, I think that's about the right price," Cass added.

"But Paul won't pay that much. He never has before," Jesse lamented.

"There are other producers that we can approach," Cass said. "I will tell him we have another producer interested."

Jesse looked at Cass. "Okay. I gave you the power to negotiate with him. Good luck."

"One other thing," Cass said. "I think we should demand that he make a demo with The Desperados singing your songs."

Howard, Lia and Jesse almost gasped simultaneously. "Wha...t?" Jesse said.

Cass nodded. "I think he may just capitulate. He can get more songs from you; he knows how prolific you are. It won't hurt him to come out with the band on his label."

"What a brazen suggestion," Howard said, looking at Cass with admiration.

"Isn't that what all the San Francisco bands do? They want to be recorded with *their* songs."

All three of them nodded as Jesse's face lit up.

"Babe, I think the best thing I ever did was put you in charge of negotiating my music."

When Paul finally arrived for a talk, Cass had told him to bring a blank contract. He huffed his portly frame up the gangplank and sat at the picnic table on deck.

Paul greeted Jesse and Cass. Howard and Lia were not there. "What did you want in the contract?" Paul asked, crossly.

"Here's the deal, Paul. Jesse will sell the two songs, *Napa County Circus Blues* and *Only Love*, to you *if* you cut a record with The Desperados singing these two songs, plus some of Jesse's old ones. Then Jesse will write two or more new ones that he will give you exclusive rights to buy for one of your name musicians."

Paul swallowed hard. "Why are you demanding such a difficult deal?" I can compensate him very well for the two songs. I have a couple of name artists who need some new music to record."

"We'll put a time element on completion of the next new songs. Jesse, can you write them in say a month's time?"Cass turned to Jesse.

"No problem," Jesse said.

Paul looked dejected at Cass. "You drive a hard bargain, young lady. Okay, I'll record The Desperados with Jesse's material and expect the new material in a month's time. Of course, you realize with having to foot the cost of a record for the band, I can't pay very much for the next songs?"

"In the contract, you will pay Jesse $500 per song in addition to the demo, unless a new negotiation occurs." Cass was enjoying this. "Once The Desperados have a record, others can record Jesse's two songs, *Only Love* and *Napa County Circus Blues.*"

"No way," Paul shook his head. "That's way too much money for an unknown."

"Okay," Cass said. "We have another producer in San Francisco who's interested in Jesse's material. We'll contact him."

Paul's eyes nearly bugged out of his head. "You've been in contact with another producer?"

"You should realize The Desperados have been playing to packed audiences in Sausalito these last few months. Word filtered over to San Francisco, I guess. He contacted us."

"Who is he?" Paul demanded.

"I'm not at liberty to tell you that, Paul. I don't want you badgering him to leave Jesse alone."

Paul sat slumped at the table. Finally he looked up at Cass and Jesse.

"Okay. I'll draw-up the contract and be back. How about tomorrow? Can you sign it then?" He looked at Jesse.

Jesse was silent. Cass answered. "Tomorrow is fine. Jesse will be paid for the two songs when he signs the contract. When do you think you can schedule the recording?"

"I can press the vinyl Sunday morning." Paul answered.

"The band has a show Friday and Saturday, so early Sunday is not good. Can we all meet at say three in the afternoon?"

Paul nodded. He picked up the blank contract and stood to leave.

"Do you remember all that we want included in the contract, or do you need me to jot it down for you?"

"I can remember." Paul left without a goodbye.

"He has this great recording studio in Berkeley," Jesse said. "It has a fine sound. We are damn lucky, and he is paying me $1000 for the two songs! This is bitchin'."

He picked up Cass in his arms. "You are some woman. How'd you do that? You just told him what he was going to do and he agreed."

"I used to be a newspaper reporter. I do know a little about people and how to manipulate them." She laughed as he swung her around.

Howard and Lia came out from the galley. They had heard Paul leave. "Sounds like you cornered him," Howard said to Cass.

"We did," Cass said. "He agreed to a demo and $500 per song until the price goes up."

"I think you found a hidden talent, Cass," Lia said. Maybe you should extend your music negotiations to other musicians."

"Not a chance," Jesse said. "She's my manager, and songbird and old lady. No one else gets any of her talent."

Cass was inwardly tickled that Jesse thought she was his possession. But for now, it was all right.

"Okay, how about Ondine's for lunch to celebrate my great luck? Lunch is on me," Jesse said.

They all grabbed shoes, Howie and Nancy, and headed for Howard's van.

18

*J*esse talked to Bartok and told him he needed a bouncer/bodyguard type to satisfy Cass's concerns about the groupies.

"I know a guy who does that sort of thing, but he's not cheap," Bartok said. "He's a Hell's Angel and pretty rough. Want to meet him?"

Jesse said that he did and a meeting was set up on The Ark for the next day.

It was a gorgeous day in Sausalito; the sun was spilling down on the deck of the Van Damme, creating abstract patterns between the shadows of the riggings. Sea gulls were hawking their sharp vocals while the sounds of Bob Dylan wafted across the houseboat community.

Kasim was Turkish and a Hell's Angel to boot. He wore his mustache in a handle-bar style and his hair was long and scraggily. He rode up on his bike in a cloud of dust. He stepped off, slapped down the kick-stand and came loudly up the gangplank to where Bartok, Howard, Lia, Jesse and Cass were seated at the picnic table and various deck chairs. Nancy and Howie were on the deck coloring.

Bartok introduced Kasim, explaining they were a band and wanted some protection during the shows so the groupies didn't mob them.

"I should have that problem," Kasim said with a crooked smile showing yellow and jagged teeth. A strip of bandana was wound around his forehead Willie Nelson style. He wore several gold chains, a leather vest with nothing underneath and blue jeans that had several rips and holes. He clomped to a chair in his heavy boots.

"I can be at your gigs on Friday and Saturday nights, stopping the pretty little chicks that are wantin' a piece of the action."

Cass spoke up. "We don't want them hurt in any way. I just want them to stay away from Jesse. I think the other guys don't mind having them hang on them."

Kasim looked from Jesse to Cass and astutely sized up the situation. "I hear ya', girl. You don't want them hangin' on your ole man. Right?"

Cass nodded.

"How do you feel about this, Jesse?" Kasim looked at him carefully.

"I really don't like to be pulled and hugged right after a gig," Jesse admitted. "I'm all sweaty and I just want to get back to the dressing room and light up a joint."

"Okay, no problem. I'll be gentle but persuasive."

They agreed to pay Kasim $60 a gig, so Jesse wasn't making any money, but he figured he had to do this to keep Cass happy and in the band.

They told Kasim when and where the next gig was and he agreed to be there at the beginning.

He got back on his bike and roared off for the city in a cloud of smoke and dirt.

Howard was mending well and soon he put up his crutches. Nancy and Howie seemed to thrive on the boat; there was always something to do, and lots of interesting people who came around.

Howard inquired about Faye at the Napa Hospital. The reports were that she was not getting better and usually dwelled in a state of confusion. Her shrink told Howard that she was pretty messed up and needed a lot of help. She would be there for quite a while.

Howard, Bartok, Jesse, Lia and Cass piled into the VW van and headed for the city to clean out Faye's apartment, while the boys in the band watched Nancy and Howie.

They picked up all the toys, kid's bedding and clothes in two sacks, stashed them in the van and collected all the rest of the linens, dishes, and furniture in a circle in the middle of the living room. Howard called the Salvation Army and they sent a truck to pick up everything. It took all day and once the apartment was cleaned, they left. One stop at a pizza parlor to pick up two combos and they returned to Sausalito and unloaded the toys.

It was a big event for Howie and Nancy. Howard spilled the sacks onto the deck of the Van Damme. The kids had forgotten most of them and felt like it was Christmas getting new toys. Howard called Faye's landlord and arranged for the return of the cleaning fee.

Bartok had heard from Jesse's parents, Etta and George only once since Jesse's visit. Etta called to say they were leaving Napa for Bellingham, Washington and would Bartok please let Jesse know.

Bartok did that but Jesse was fully engrossed in his new career with his folk-rock band. He hardly gave a thought to his parents, or his sister. They were not part of his life anymore.

The recording in Berkeley at Paul's studio went well. The vinyl was pressed and the demo was given to Jesse and the band. If they wanted albums made from the demo it would cost. They had decided to wait a while before paying anyone to produce albums.

Jesse took the demo to a sound engineer he knew at KPFK radio and he began playing the demo on the air. Soon Jesse's songs became known to the fans that listened to the station.

The Desperados continued to play on the boat every night but Friday and Saturdays, when usually after midnight they would traipse onto the Van Damme and set up in The Ark coffee house and play again until three or four in the morning. Cass was getting used to this life, but she was also tired a lot. She didn't get enough sleep, though Jesse seemed to do just fine on four or five hours sleep a night.

One sun-filled morning in June Cass was sitting on deck drying her hair. The seagulls were singing their songs and the wind blew gently through her locks. Jesse walked up the gangplank and announced the new gig he had arranged. "I got us booked into the North Beach Club next Saturday," he told Cass. The North Beach Club was *the* place to play in San Francisco, right next to Caffe Trieste on Vallejo Street.

"Cool, do the guys know yet?" she asked.

"Nope. You're the first one I've told."

"That's bitchin'. How'd you pull that off?"

"I played the demo and mentioned KPFK was playing it. They liked the music so they gave us a one night booking."

Cass was happy for Jesse. He sat beside her and kissed her. Lia and Howard came out of the wheel house and when Jesse told them the news they congratulated him, too.

"We want to be there for your debut performance at the North Beach Club," Howard said.

"I'll see if I can get Bartok to babysit."

Bartok was fine with taking care of Nancy and Howie so the next Friday night the band and Howard and Lia drove over to the club in North Beach. The neighborhood was a series of small clubs, hip bars and art galleries. They arrived at 9 p.m. and the band set up.

Cass was nervous about remembering all of the words, but Jesse had written them out for her in a notebook. She hummed all the way over, trying to keep the tunes in her head.

"Don't sweat it, babe, you'll do just fine," Jesse assured her.

When the music finally started, the club was packed. Jesse and The Desperados played an instrumental and then he started the song, *Only Love*, one of his new ones. Cass harmonized on it and suddenly the club quieted down. When the song was over, the audience exploded in applause, making Cass and the band feel welcomed.

Cass and Jesse interacted on the next few songs, he standing next to her and the mike and playing his twelve string. She holding on to the microphone stand and leaning in toward him. John walked over to the sound display and adjusted the levels. All of the band members seemed to be in perfect sync.

John on keyboard, David on bass guitar and Spence on drums made for a grand blend. After each song the audience went wild, and then, about the time Cass's voice started to give out, it was over.

The manager of the club came back to the dressing room. "Can you guys come back tomorrow night? We loved your music and apparently so did the crowd out front."

Jesse looked at the guys in the band. Everyone nodded in a low key manner. "Sure we can be here tomorrow night," Jesse said.

"I'm gonna' talk to my partner. We may want to book you for the next month. Can you do that?" the manager asked. "Of course, we'll make an adjustment on the bread."

Again Jesse made eye contact with three guys. They all nodded. "I think we can rearrange our schedule," Jesse said.

When the manager left, the guys whooped and lit up a joint. "Man, we're on our way," David said.

"Let's don't get overconfident," Spence said. "This is just our first big gig."

"What are we gonna' ask for in pay, Jesse?" John asked.

"We need to contact some other bands and see what they are getting," Jesse answered.

"I know a couple of the guys in the We Five band. I'll ask them what bands are getting paid."

"Fab," David said.

On the way home, Cass was subdued. The success of the band sort of overwhelmed her and she wanted life to slow down.

"You okay?" Jesse asked, glancing at her from the driver's seat.

She nodded. "Just wondering where this is going, the band and my singing with you guys."

"Don't worry so much. Just hang loose, babe. You did great tonight. We sang really cool together on *Love Only*." He blew her a kiss.

When they got back to the Van Damme the band set up for another set. Cass bowed out. "I'm going to bed," she said to Jesse.

"Okay, babe. I may crawl in with you later." He kissed her and she went below to her room.

She didn't pull the trunk against the door, just fell into the bunk and was asleep immediately.

In the morning when the sun peeked through the porthole, she turned over and Jesse was not there.

19

Cass dressed and went up on deck. Lia and Howard were having their morning coffee. Cass poured herself a cup from the galley and sat down across from them on the picnic table. Howard wouldn't look at her and Lia stared into her eyes.

The three of them watched Jesse walk a young woman off his boat and down the dock to Bridgeway. She stuck out her thumb for a ride and he left her there. On the way back, Jesse saw them on deck and came up the gangplank.

When he sat down next to Cass, she got up. "Babe, I'm sorry. That's just the way I am."

Lia and Howard were silent; respecting Jesse and Cass's space.

"Stay away from me," she said. Red lights flashing from her eyes.

"Look, I told you how it was with me."

"And I'm telling you how it is with me. Stay away from me. Don't even talk to me. I'm through with you and the band." Cass stormed below deck to her room.

She couldn't think what she should do. Pack up and leave? Maybe that would be best. She started throwing things into her suitcase. There was a knock on the door.

"Go away."

"Cass, it's me, Lia."

Cass didn't answer, so Lia opened the door. "What are you doing, packing?"

"Yes, I'm splitting."

"Where will you go?"

"I don't know yet. I just want to get away from him. Maybe I'll catch a bus back to L.A."

"Honey, you knew Jesse was like that."

Suddenly Cass dissolved into tears. "Yes, I knew. I just believed him when he said I meant something to him."

"You do mean something to him. He can care more about you and still have a few young things on the side."

"I don't want to be in a relationship like that. I don't want to be in the band anymore. He took all the joy out of it for me."

"Then don't, but stay here and we will have a nice summer in spite of Jesse."

Cass wiped her tears and sat on the bunk. Maybe she wouldn't split right now. Maybe she'd think about it.

"Maybe," She said.

Lia sat beside her and put her arm around her waist. "Men can be animals, but we don't have to allow them to hurt us," Lia said.

Cass wiped her eyes and let Lia lead her back on deck. Jesse was still sitting at the table with Howard. He looked at Cass carefully. Cass sat on a deck chair and Lia went over to Howard. "We had a talk and she is staying for the time being. But she is through with the band." She looked at Jesse. "You'll have to get another girl singer."

"Aw...Cass. We can still do the band. You are such a great singer."

Cass said nothing and wouldn't even look at Jesse.

"We have this boss gig over in North Beach, for a month. Sure you won't stay with the band?"

Cass still wouldn't speak to Jesse.

He stood. "I'll tell the guys. They won't be happy. They love having you sing with us." He walked over to Cass. "Can we declare a truce?" he held out his hand.

She ignored him and looked the other way.

"Okay." He walked down the gangplank and down the dock to his boat.

⌐

Claire was selling tickets for the Big Top. They had been in Bellingham for two weeks and there were going to be there another month. She hated it here; so cold and the wind blew all the time. If only she could walk she would leave this place.

She had been trying at night when everyone was asleep, to get out of bed and struggle to the wheel chair a few feet away. Putting each foot down in front of the other was a difficult task. Right now she half-dragged them and supported her upper body with her arms. Someone had given her a sturdy walker and she had been using that to get to her chair. Once she had made it and she felt a tiny glimmer of hope that she might be able to use her legs again. She would keep trying and if one day she could get to the chair on her own, easily, she was gone. Her parents had kept her dependent on them; she knew it was part sympathy and part guilt. She needed to get away from them. She wanted to go to Sausalito and visit Jesse.

ↄ

Sometimes when the drugs had almost worn off Faye could think a little more clearly. She remembered Howie and Nancy, her children. Where were they? Who was caring for them? She'd ask the shrink next time she saw him.

Faye went to the window and saw that summer was still in full bloom. The hydrangeas were still a gorgeous blue and the bougainvillea was vibrantly growing around the arbor.

Her dinner was brought; meatloaf and mashed potatoes and corn. She only ate a few bites and pushed it away. She drank all of her tea, hoping for a little zing from the caffeine, anything to remind her she was still alive and able to think.

When the nurse brought her pill she held it in her mouth behind her teeth and drank a sip of water. Distracted, the nurse didn't notice her small drink. She left with her tray and utensils. Faye immediately took out the pill and hid it beside the others she'd managed to save in one of her tampon tubes. She didn't know why she was saving them; she just didn't want to take them all the time.

ↄ

Cass was sitting on the deck of the Van Damme singing a song. John, Spence and David came up the gangplank. Cass stopped playing and laid her guitar down.

"Cass," Spence said. "We want to ask you to please come back to the band. We played last night at the North Beach Club and the manager said if we didn't return with the girl singer the deal was off. Besides that, we really want you with us. You are part of The Desperados." Spence took a deep breath.

John and David agreed. "We really miss having you up there with us," Spence said.

Cass was surprised. She hadn't thought the band would miss her at all. She remained silent.

"I want you back with us, too," John said. "We will try and help you through this trying time with Jesse. If you need us for a buffer we'll be here for you."

Cass started to cry. "I didn't realize you guys would care that much."

"We do. We all think Jesse is an ass for losing you, but that's between you and him. We just want you back in the band," John said.

Cass wiped her cheeks. "I'll think about it guys. Thanks for asking me."

"We got a gig over there in North Beach tonight. Any chance you could join us?"

"I'll let you know before you leave."

John put his hand on Cass's shoulder. "Okay. We'll be on Jesse's boat. Why don't you meet us at my van in the parking lot if you want to join us. We'll load up the instruments about 8 p.m."

Cass nodded and thanked them for coming over to ask her to rejoin the band.

Lia came out of the wheel house. "I overheard the guys asking you to sing tonight. That was real sweet of them."

"Yeah. They're a good group."

"Well?" Lia said.

"I guess I'll go. I don't have to talk to Jesse. Just sing with him."

"That may be a little awkward. You'll have to be civil to him on stage."

"I can be. I just don't want a relationship with him."

"Just try to get along while you two are together in the band."

"I will. I think Jesse will, too."

At 8 p.m. when the guys were loading up the van, Cass walked out to the parking lot and climbed in the back. Jesse smiled at her and she ignored him. John climbed in beside her and put his arm around the back of her seat. The two of them talked about the newest creation of Jesse's, *Jesse's Song*, on the way over the bridge.

⤚

Bartok continued to paint as he smoked a joint. He was finishing up on a large work measuring 3 x 5 feet. It was destined for a show in San Francisco at the Frantero Gallery.

He cleaned his brushes in the sink in soapy water, letting the acrylic paint flush down the drain and out to the Bay. He washed his hands, rubbing pieces of dried paint off his fingers. His thoughts went to Cass, Jesse and The Desperados.

He knew about Cass and Jesse's troubles; he felt personally that Jesse did not treasure Cass, but it wasn't his business and he hesitated to say anything. If he were asked, he would give that young pup, Jesse a good lecture, but he was not consulted so he tried to keep his mouth closed. Young people these days didn't seem to consider each other's feelings. Yes, he knew this was the new moral freedom, to take sexual gratification whenever and wherever it became opportune. But one must still consider the feelings of those involved. He knew Cass was terribly hurt and probably would not forgive Jesse. Maybe this was a lesson Jesse needed to learn.

He cleaned up and got ready to go over to the city to hear The Desperados play tonight. He had baby-sat the kids for Howard and Lia both weekends that the band played in North Beach. Now it was his turn.

Slipping on his clean trousers, a tie-dye shirt and sandals, he locked up his boat, climbed in his VW bug and headed over to San Francisco.

20

$\mathcal{L}$ia fixed dinner for Howie and Nancy and she and Howard sat in deck chairs while they ate.

"I kind of wished we were going to the city to listen to the band," lamented Lia. "I guess Cass will be okay. It sounded like the guys will look out for her and be a buffer between her and Jesse if needed."

"I think Cass will be fine once her broken heart begins to mend. This happens to all of us. She just wasn't ready for sharing her man."

"Cass will never be," Lia said. "I know her. She split from her husband because he was having an affair with his secretary."

"Life has a way of teaching us the lessons we need to learn," Howard offered.

"Have you heard anything from the hospital in Napa about Faye?" Lia asked in a quiet voice.

"Not for a week or so. Her shrink, Dr. Lambert said she is becoming less foggy. She asked about the children and the doc told her they were here with me."

"How did that affect her?"

"Apparently she is okay with that. If she gets out of Napa she will have to stand trial for attempted murder. I don't think she wants that."

"Daddy, I want to play paper dolls," Nancy piped up.

"Go get them from your room," Howard said.

When Nancy came back she and Howard sat on the deck and started dressing them.

Lia began laughing. "I never thought I'd see you in this position."

"Come on, Nancy, let's get up and sit at the table," Howard said.

Howard and Nancy picked up the paper toys and transferred them to the picnic table.

"I want to do something," Howie whined.

"Let's go down and look at the boats," Lia said.

"Okay," Howie agreed immediately, hopping off the picnic bench and running for the gangplank.

"Wait for me, Howie," Lia called.

Howard watched his son and his 'old lady' ambling down the dock looking at the boats.

⤙

Claire packed a soft satchel with two changes of clothes, her pain medication and took the money she had saved from the dresser. She wrote a short note to her parents.

> I'm leaving. I don't want to be here anymore. Don't
> worry, I'll be fine.
> Love, Claire

Etta and George were in the Big Tent practicing for the show tonight. One look around the trailer told her she could shed this place without a moment's regret. She opened the door and placed her wheelchair carefully on the ramp of their trailer and slowing with the brake on, made her way down the ramp to the ground. She wheeled herself two blocks to the Bellingham bus station.

Once inside the terminal, she wheeled up to a window and bought a ticket for Sausalito, California. The woman behind the window looked at her strangely. "Are you goin' by yourself, dearie?" she asked.

"Yes," Claire answered.

"Can you manage that?"

"Of course, otherwise I wouldn't be going."

"The bus has a lift to take your chair onto the vehicle. You won't have a problem there," the woman informed her.

"Thank you, I knew that," Claire answered.

She rested beside a bench for an hour until a bus for California pulled into the station. Then she wheeled out to the bus and the driver using the power-lift took her on board.

He placed her wheelchair just behind his seat in a space designed for wheelchairs.

Claire was torn with conflicting emotions. She wanted away from her parents and this restrictive life, but she knew Jesse may not want a crippled sister to take care of. If she worked every day as she had been to strengthen her legs, maybe eventually she could walk with a walker or crutches. That was her goal. To be able to get around on her own, without the wheelchair all the time. She didn't care what the doctors said. She had a determination and strength they knew nothing about.

Finally the bus was loaded and it began its long, two-day trip to Sausalito. Claire knew she would have to sleep in her chair and getting off at stops for the bathroom would be a chore, but she was determined to go to her brother, Jesse.

～

Howard was healing fast. He no longer had to use his crutches. He got back into the swing of the music, food, drink and drugs every night on the boat. He was becoming more attached to Lia and dependent on her for the care of his two children. He would begin divorce proceedings with Faye, as soon as he could. He wanted a life with Lia.

He stretched himself out on the deck chair and began his exercises to strengthen his arm.

Jesse and Kayak came up on deck. "Is Cass around?"

"No, she and Lia went to town. What's up?"

"I just wanted to see if she'd talk to me. We had a pretty good show last night in North Beach. She and I were harmonizing beautifully and she even smiled at me."

"Jesse, you hurt her pretty bad. I wouldn't expect her to forgive you anytime soon," Howard said.

"Man, I know. I'm really sorry I hurt her. I didn't realize it meant so much to her, being faithful. You know, the other chicks, they don't care or want more than a one-night stand."

"Cass is different. Some women still want one man at a time and they expect the same. Why don't you leave Cass alone and keep on with your usual groupies?"

"I can't get her out of my head. Especially singing with her every night."

"Go easy with her. Just let time heal. Maybe in a few weeks she'll forgive you, maybe she never will."

Jesse sat down next to Howard. Kayak lay down beside his chair. "How's it going with you and Lia?"

"Good. I don't let her see me looking elsewhere and I'm only looking, not doing. I learned a valuable lesson with Faye."

"Guess I could learn a lesson or two from you. I just can't seem to keep from being turned on by the young chicks that hang around."

"Being turned on is one thing, just don't act on those feelings," Howard said.

"Yeah…if I want Cass back, I guess that's what I have to do."

Jesse pulled out a joint and he and Howard sat and smoked in silence.

⌐

John came on the Van Damme and saw Cass sitting on deck feeding the gulls. He went over and sat beside her. "HI. I thought if you're not busy we could get some lunch together downtown."

"That would be nice. Let me finish up with this old bread. The gulls really like it."

"Sure," John responded. "What did you think of the performance last night?"

Cass turned to look at him. "I think it went well. The audience seemed to like it. What do you think?"

"I thought you and Jesse harmonized really well together. I am going to suggest that you and he seem more involved on stage. Maybe look at each other now and then when you're singing."

Cass gave him a direct look. "Why do you suggest that? Do we not seem involved with our music?"

"Yes and no. There is a definite coldness between the two of you and it reflects on stage."

"I'm sorry that I can't do anything about that. It's just the way I feel."

"When you're on stage you are an actor as well as singer. You can pretend that you and Jesse are good friends."

"I didn't think we sent the opposite message to the audience. Have you talked to Jesse about this?"

"No, just you."

"If I start acting like I'm warming up to Jesse, he will get the wrong idea."

"Not if you tell him it's an act."

Cass thought about this for a minute. "I guess I could try to act more warmly to him on stage."

"Good. Where would you like to eat lunch?"

"I don't care. Where ever you want."

"How 'bout we celebrate and go to Valhalla's?"

"What's the occasion?"

"Just our success at the North Beach Club."

"Sounds good to me. Let me tell Lia I'm gone, so she won't expect me to stay with the children."

Cass disappeared into the galley and she and Lia came out together. "You're taking Cass out to lunch? Don't let Jesse hear about it."

"It's just a friendly lunch, Lia. Nothing more to it than that," John said.

"Besides Jesse no longer has a say in what I do," Cass said.

"Right." John took her arm and they walked down the gangplank to his van.

⤵

Faye was having her sixth session with her shrink, Dr. Lambert. She shuffled into the office and sat in one of the comfortable sofa-chairs. Faye had been stock-piling her pills so she was fairly clear-headed this morning.

"Good morning, Faye," Dr. Lambert said.

"Hi," Faye said.

"We left off last time with you telling me why you thought you shot your husband. Do you still feel that way?"

Faye remembered. "Yes. I was furious at him and wanted to hurt him. I don't think I thought it out to what shooting him would mean. I really didn't want him dead or hurt. I wanted to hurt him emotionally."

"What are your feelings now about your children?"

"I'm glad they are staying with Howard. I know that means they are also with his mistress but hopefully she is taking good care of them. When I get out of here I want them back."

"If and when you get out of here do you realize that you will have to stand trial for attempted murder?"

Faye caught her breath. "Why? I didn't mean to kill him."

"You still assaulted him with a gun. That is the way the law works. If you get well enough that I think you can leave, you will stand trial."

Faye was silent. "How much time would I get for that?"

"It's up to a judge. They can give you the maximum or the minimum sentence."

"What would that be?"

"It varies from judge to judge, but I would expect you would only have to be in prison from 5 to 10 years. Especially since you didn't mean to kill Howard."

"My kids would be grown up by then." Faye's face was grief-stricken.

"One of the signposts of getting well is realizing there are consequences for our behavior," the doctor said sagely.

"If they continue to give me those pills I will never get well. It creates a fog in my brain."

"Yes. I'm sorry about that. I think you are ready to go off those pills and we'll put you on another regime."

"What regime would that be?"

"I think we can give you something that gives you energy and an optimistic frame of mind."

That sounded good to Faye. Better than those downers.

21

$\mathcal{T}$he Desperados had finished their month's gig in North Beach. The band members had moved into rooms below deck on the Van Damme. It was a Friday night and some of the band was playing in The Ark coffee house. Cass was not singing with them at the moment, she was standing next to the punch bowl in the galley. She picked up a paper cup and slipped it into the red punch. John came up behind her and took the cup from her hand. "You probably only need a fourth of a cup of this punch. Jesse spiked the punch with LSD."

"LSD?" Cass asked.

"Acid, Sandoz acid. Apparently Tim Leary is in town and Jesse got some acid from the man himself."

"I see," realization dawning on Cass. "Thanks, John. Are you drinking some?"

"Yep," He said as he dipped his paper cup into the punch.

Bartok was right behind them as he took a cup of the punch. "Happy landings, kids," he said.

This would be the first time Cass had taken acid. She wanted to have an outstanding experience.

Shortly after Cass had drunk the punch she began feeling different. Her body felt more alive and her muscles were moving smoothly in everything she did. The colors that passed by her vision were more intense;

strong blues, pinks, reds, oranges and yellows. Her perception of the boat took on an acute awareness. She saw every dent in the deck. The paint was peeling in several places much like below in the rooms.

John guided her to an outstretched lawn chair. She lay down and he lay beside her. Her mind was floating in the Universe among angels, flying horses, people and lots of colors. Everything was distorted, including John's face, which was like a Picasso painting. She felt John put his arms around her and kiss her. She kissed him back. Her body responded naturally, which surprised her. They were kissing and embracing but that seemed to be all that was wanted by either.

A long time later, she was in her room below deck, naked and laying on her bunk. The man who was kissing her now was Jesse. He hovered over her, his hair hanging down around her face like a cloak. He was naked too, and he entered her and she felt like a larvae about to burst into a butterfly. There was a feeling of oneness with Jesse, an ecstatic joy in the sex act. She had long periods of not remembering what she was doing, but when she finally started coming down, she was still on her bunk with Jesse. The radio was playing Bob Dylan's, *Blowing in the Wind*. It took on a prophetic anthem that she was sure he meant when he wrote it. She saw blues and greens in the words of the song.

"I love you, Cass." She heard Jesse say those words. "I want you for my woman. I'm so sorry I hurt you. I won't hurt you again, I promise."

She didn't trust herself to talk, not sure if she could get a sound out. "Um...m," she mumbled.

Jesse continued to embrace her and stroke her hair and body. She twirled his hair on her finger; it was fine and soft and was made of many colors.

They stayed in her room for several hours; until the drug wore off enough to walk. Then she and Jesse dressed and went up on deck. People were locked together on deck chairs, couches, sleeping bags, whatever they could find to lay on. Others were walking around in a state of bliss.

The sun was up and the cloud cover that usually appeared in the mornings in Sausalito had lifted. Bright shafts of sun splashed across the white deck bathing the sleepers in an awesome light. Everything seemed brilliant and clear this morning, like a rain-washed day.

She went to the ice box and took out two cold sodas. She and Jesse sat at a table in the coffee house and drank them.

Before they were finished, Lia and Howard came out of the wheel house with Howie and Nancy.

"Hey, where did you two disappear to?" Howard asked.

"Downstairs," Jesse said.

Lia seated the children at the table and cut an apple for them. Howard brought a bottle of Scotch and four paper cups over.

"No thanks," Cass said.

Jesse took a shot as did Lia and Howard.

"Man that was some trip. Anybody see Bartok?" Jesse asked.

"I saw him last night. Not sure where he is now," Howard answered.

Lia went into the galley and brought back four oranges and a knife. She cut them in halves and set them in the middle of the table.

Cass's first bite was juicy, tasting of orange blossoms and cinnamon. It was full of tartness on her tongue. She sucked the orange, savoring the flavor, smelling the skin when she was finished. She wanted to hold on to the colorful, sensual feelings she had experienced on this, her first acid trip.

"Everything smells so fab," she said.

Jesse laughed fully and held his arms to the sky. "Thank you Universe, for giving me back my Princess."

Lia looked at Cass. "So you two made up?"

Cass looked back. "I guess. We ended up in the sack together."

"Try to not make the same mistake again, Jesse, hang loose," Howard warned, but smiled as he spoke.

"Oh I'll be damn sure not to mess up again," Jesse said.

⌐

Bartok answered the phone. He heard a female voice on the other end. "Hello, is this Bartok?"

"It is. Who's calling?"

"This is Claire, Jesse's sister. Is he still living near you in Sausalito?"

Bartok hesitated, but finally said, "Yes."

"I'm downtown in Sausalito and I wonder if you could tell Jesse I'm at the Tides Book Store. I'd like to see him. Would you do that, please?"

Bartok was surprised, but said, "Of course, I'll get in touch with him right away. You just stay there."

He hung up and sat down. Life was getting complicated for Jesse these days, he thought. Now his crippled sister was in town wanting to see him.

Bartok went next door to Jesse's boat. He stepped on board and called down to the cabin. When he got no answer he opened the door and went below. No one was there but Kayak. The dog greeted him with enthusiasm. He left Jesse's boat and walked to the Van Damme and found Lia and Howard, on the deck with the kids.

"Anyone seen Jesse?" Bartok asked.

"He went with Cass down to the beach. What's up," Howard asked.

"His sister is waiting at the Tides Book Store and wants to see him."

Howard whistled. "Man...how did she get here? I thought she was disabled and used a wheelchair?"

"She is and she does. I didn't ask her how she got here. She asked me to get a hold of Jesse. Guess I'll go down and pick her up. Can I bring her back here?"

Howard nodded. "Don't see why not. We'll find some place for her."

"Do you want me to go with you, Bartok?" Lia asked.

"Sure, come along."

"You get to entertain the children," Lia said to Howard.

Bartok and Lia went in Howard's VW van. They pulled up in front of the Tides and Lia got out while Bartok pulled into the parking lot across the street.

Once inside the book store, they looked for a young woman that fit the description of Claire. They knew she was a fine looking chick with long black hair. It only took a quick look around to see Claire sitting at a table drinking a cup of Espresso.

Lia and Bartok approached her table. "Claire?" Bartok asked.

She smiled and nodded. "Yes, I thought Jesse was coming."

"I couldn't find Jesse. I think he went to the beach," Bartok said.

"Oh." Claire looked down at the table. "I guess I'll just stay here or across the street in the park until he gets back and you can tell him."

"Hi, I'm Lia. I live on the Van Damme with my boyfriend, Howard. He's the captain. There's plenty of room on the Van Damme so we thought we'd take you to the boat. Jesse's sailboat is tied up just down the pier."

Claire looked at Lia. "That's very kind of you. Okay."

Bartok scratched his forehead. "Say, how did you get here from Bellingham?"

"I took a greyhound from there to here."

Lia and Bartok both nodded. "I see," said Bartok.

"They had a lift that took my chair on board. The bus driver was very nice to me. He lowered me on the lift when I needed to use the bathroom. Some of the women escorted me to the Ladies Room and brought me food. When the driver changed the new one was very nice, too. I didn't want for anything, except privacy." Claire laughed.

"Well, you could do an ad for the Greyhound Bus Lines," Lia said with a smile.

Claire grinned.

"I'm going to go get the van and park right in front of the book store," Bartok said. "Lia you bring Claire out and between the two of us we'll lift her into the front seat."

"I can lift myself into the car. I'm quite strong and my legs are working a little."

"Ok," Bartok said and he turned and left.

"That's far-out that you're legs are working," Lia said.

"Yes, I've been working on them even before Jesse visited us at the Napa Fair Grounds.

My goal is to be able to use a walker."

"That's cool," Lia said.

Claire left money on the table and they headed for the door. Bartok was waiting in Howard's van right in front with the car door open. Claire wheeled over to the passenger seat, put on the brakes, and lifted herself into the car.

Bartok put the wheelchair in the back of the van with Claire's satchel and they headed for the Van Damme.

Bartok pushed the chair up the gangplank with Howard's help. Once on deck, Claire saw Jesse and Cass sitting at a table. Jesse got up and walked to Claire. Howard and Lia stood watching.

"Girl...what are you doing here?" He didn't seem all that happy to see her.

"I took a greyhound bus from Bellingham. I was tired of the circus and I wanted to see you."

Jesse just shook his head like he had trouble believing all this was happening.

"Aren't you glad to see me," she asked, her eyes starting to fill.

Cass got up and crossed to Claire. "Of course, he is. We're happy to see you. Just surprised that you could make the trip all by yourself."

Jesse leaned down and kissed Claire on the cheek. "Yeah, I'm just surprised."

"Come on over here to the table. Are you hungry?" Cass asked.

"Sort of," Claire said.

Lia and Cass went to the galley and fixed a peanut butter and jelly sandwich. Lia brought it back to Claire with an Orange Soda.

"How long are you planning on staying?" Jesse asked.

"Not sure, but I'm not going back."

Jesse looked shocked. "You can't get along without Mom and Dad taking care of you."

"I think I can. I can walk a little. I've been working hard on my legs and I can drag them some. Here I'll show you." Claire moved slowly from the wheelchair to the bench of the picnic table, using her hands and arms to support herself.

Cass laughed. "You did good, girl."

"Bitchin," Howard echoed.

Jesse sat beside her and took her hand. "I'm not sure we can give you the care you need here."

"You don't want me here, is that it?" Her eyes began to tear again.

"Of course we want you here," Cass said. Lia agreed.

"Hey, we'll do what is necessary for you to stay," Howard said. "Jesse will help, too." He glared at his friend.

Howie and Nancy spilled out of the wheel house having wakened from their naps. "Daddy, Lia," Nancy said. Howie rubbed his eyes. "I'm hungry."

"When are these kids not hungry," Lia said, standing and going to the galley to fix them some lunch.

Everyone laughed to relieve the tension that had built up on deck. Claire forgot her distress and asked about the children. Cass told her who they were.

"We certainly have a diverse group here," Howard said.

John, David and Spence came up on deck and were introduced to Claire. David suggested going to the Kettle Deli and picking up a couple of pizzas for lunch. Everyone threw in a few dollars and David split for the deli.

⌐

Jesse took Cass aside one evening before the music started on The Ark. "I don't want you going out with John. You're my old lady."

Cass looked at him in amazement. "Now, Jesse, you can't manage my life. I'm still a single girl and if I want to have lunch with John, I will."

"He has a hankering' for you, I don't like that," Jesse said. "He was kissing you when we dropped acid."

"I think I was kissing him back. I was not connected to you then. Get over your jealousy. It isn't attractive."

"But now you're my old lady and I don't want him thinking he can horn in on my territory."

"You have a double standard. It's okay for you to have groupies, but I can't have a friend to go to lunch with?"

"Is he only a friend?"

"Yes, that's all he is."

Jesse sat quietly for a moment. "Okay. I still don't like it, but I guess I can't stop you."

Cass stroked his shoulder and back. "Don't sweat it, Jesse. Everything's okay."

Jesse pulled Cass up by her hand. "Let's go down to your room, babe."

Cass allowed him to lead her below deck.

22

$\mathcal{H}$oward found a small room on deck that was used as a storage room. He and Lia and Cass emptied the room of the things stored there and deposited them in other places on the boat. Lia and Cass cleaned the room and Jesse and Howard gave a fresh coat of paint to the walls. Jesse visited the Salvation Army and found a dresser and overstuffed chair and brought them back to the Van Damme. They dragged a bunk bed from the lower deck to the new room. Lia and Cass made up the bed and showed Claire where she would be staying.

When Claire saw the room she was stunned. "I didn't mean for anyone to go to so much trouble. I could have slept on a sleeping bag in the coffee house." Moisture began to form in her eyes.

"We wanted you to be comfortable," Cass said.

"I'm sure I will be in here. Thank you all soooooo much!" She gave her big brother a hug and blew a kiss to Cass, Lia and Howard.

"If you need anything let us know," Howard said.

"We put you near the galley so you can get to it easily. The toilet is just around the corner," Lia said.

⤳

The Desperados were back performing at the Tides Book Store and Coffee Shop Friday and Saturday nights. Cass and Jesse were making beautiful music together. John backed off from taking Cass to lunch since she and Jesse were back together.

"We need to practice this afternoon and decide what we're playing tonight," Jesse said.

Before Jesse could go below and tell the band members, Bartok came trudging up the gangplank. "I brought a painting to hang in Claire's room so she will have something on her walls." Bartok showed everyone a picture of the San Francisco skyline and the Bay.

"It's beautiful," Claire said. "Cass, do we have a nail so we could put it up now?"

Howard went to a drawer in the galley and a got a picture hanger and a hammer. He went into Claire's room and he and Bartok hung the painting.

"All the comforts of home and more..." Bartok joked.

Claire wiped the tears away. "You are all so kind; I don't know what to say. This is a million times more comfortable than ...back at the circus."

Howard put on an album of Simon and Garfunkel and lit a joint. "Time to celebrate Claire's arrival," he said.

John, Spence and David came up from below deck. They sent another joint in the opposite direction. When the joint came to Claire she didn't know what to do with it.

"Have you never smoked before?" Jesse asked.

She shook her head.

"Time you learned." He took a hit and blew it into her open mouth just as he had done with Cass on the first night they had met. Claire received the smoke, coughed but let Jesse blow smoke into her mouth a second time.

"I think I'm feeling it," she said with a lovely smile on her face.

Howard went into the wheel house and brought out a bong. He shaved some hash off a large ball and laid it in the bowl. It was lit and everyone partook of the bong. After one hit Claire declined. "I'm already really stoned," she said laughing.

"That's the best way to take each day," Jesse said. "Let's go over to my boat and practice. Who's coming?" The band members all followed Jesse.

"Do you want to go to Jesse's boat, Claire?" Cass asked.

"I would but I'm not sure I can get on the boat."

"Don't worry about that," Cass said as she pushed Claire down the gangplank.

When they got to Jesse's sailboat everyone had gone down in the cabin. "Hey, someone come help me get Claire aboard," Cass called out.

John and Jesse came up on deck and lifted her wheel chair onto the sailboat. "I'm not sure we can get the chair down the steps," Jesse said, stopping at the cabin entrance.

"No problem," John said. He swiftly picked up Claire in his arms before she could protest and climbed down the stairs setting her on the couch.

"That was a smooth move," Cass said, smiling.

"It took my breath away," Claire said, "it happened so fast."

Everyone started tuning up and soon the music began. Claire was fascinated and loved every minute of it.

The Desperados spent the afternoon practicing some of Jesse's new songs while Claire listened attentively on the couch.

⌒

Jesse borrowed Howard's van and drove to Berkeley with Claire and Cass. "I want to show you girls Berkeley. It's the sweetest little town. Very liberal and progressive with lots of open minded people who live there… and besides there's the University."

Neither Cass nor Claire had been there. Jesse drove into the town after crossing the San Rafael Bridge from Marin. He turned up University Avenue and drove to the Cal campus.

"We can walk around and go over to Telegraph Avenue, where all the hippies hang out," he said.

Jesse parked and he and Cass got Claire organized in her wheelchair and began walking. The campus was huge, and they headed toward Telegraph Avenue. Several free spirited individuals were standing on corners preaching, proselytizing, ranting, and some were even educating the people on the street. Jesse pointed out Mario Salvo on the steps of a University building, shouting for free speech.

Claire was engrossed in this new experience. She hardly knew anything about political activism, or even the hippie movement. She had read about the new move toward sexual freedom, but was not really aware of what that meant.

They visited Cody's Bookstore on Telegraph; Jesse bought *The Doors of Perception* by Aldus Huxley and they had lunch at a middle-eastern restaurant across the street. Walking into the restaurant the aroma of curry and turmeric made Cass's mouth water. Claire loved the stuffed grape leaves with curried pilaf and the cucumber yogurt salad she was served. Cass enjoyed the same. Jesse ordered Espresso and baklava, for dessert.

When they left the restaurant they pushed Claire's wheelchair the three blocks on Telegraph and visited all the shops. The weather was typical Berkeley; warm but overcast. Claire bought a pair of silver earrings and Cass bought a beaded necklace from a vendor in front of one of the shops.

When they headed back to the van, Claire slept all the way back to Sausalito. Cass and Jesse talked quietly in front. "Thank you for the nice tour," Cass said, kissing Jesse's cheek.

"It was cool. I loved showing my two favorite chicks around town."

"Are we playing tonight at The Ark?" Cass asked.

"Spence is over in San Francisco tonight playing with another band but I think we can jam. Why, what did you have in mind?"

"I was just hoping we could go to bed a little earlier than we usually do. I'm so tired lately."

Jesse looked at her carefully. "You're not pregnant, are you?"

Cass shook her head. "No, I'm just tired."

⁓

Faye walked down the hall to her shrink appointment. An attendant was right behind her. As if she could escape with all the bars on the windows and doors.

Dr. Lambert sat in her chair staring out the window. When Faye took a seat the doctor swiveled around in her chair and greeted her.

"Good morning Faye. How are you feeling?"

"The same," Faye said. "Caged and angry about it."

"I have some news for you. Dr. Phillips and I have discussed your progress and with you being on the new anti-depressants, we were thinking you might be ready to be released."

Dr Phillips had examined her last week and asked her a lot of questions. Faye looked shocked. "You mean I can go home and have my kids with me?"

Dr. Lambert looked down. "Not exactly. Since we will have to make a statement for the courts that you are no longer disturbed, they will most likely charge you with attempted murder and put you on trial."

Faye sat in the chair stunned. She contemplated the news. "But I didn't mean to shoot to kill him; I was just so hurt." Faye began to cry.

"That is something you need to tell your lawyer. Do you have one?"

Faye shook her head.

"I will contact your husband and he can visit you here and perhaps help you get a lawyer." The doctor handed Faye a tissue. She took it and wiped her eyes and blew her nose.

On the way back to her room, Faye felt a sudden heavy gloom envelop her. She didn't know how she ended up in this terrible situation. Howard was her husband and she didn't want to kill him. Her life was spiraling out of control. There was a definite improvement in her attitude since she's been on anti-depressants. She'd been pretty cheerful of late, but this news that she would have to stand trial was devastating. The attendant unlocked her room and escorted Faye inside. She smiled at her and left, locking the door on the outside.

Faye thought she had been in denial about a trial. Maybe Howard would testify for her that she didn't mean to hurt him. But Howard had a new girlfriend and he was no longer interested in her or her life. He had their kids and his mistress and he didn't need anything from Faye. She sat on her bed and let the tears seep down her cheeks. She really had no life anymore. It was either being caged in this lunatic facility or prison. She knew she would be convicted of trying to kill Howard. Who would believe her? She only knew of one escape.

She found the socks rolled up at the bottom of her dresser drawer and counted out the 36 pills she had managed to save.

She picked up her plastic cup of water, put all of the pills in her mouth, and drank all of the water. Faye lay back on her bed and waited for sleep to shroud her like a winding sheet. Good bye sweet Howie and Nancy. I'll always love you, she thought.

23

*J*ohn and Claire had been dating. Jesse was relieved but concerned too. He didn't want his sister hurt. He found John reading on the deck of the Van Damme one morning and he cornered him.

"John, I don't know your intentions toward my sister, but I don't want her hurt. When you are through with her what happens to her?"

John looked up from his book. "Jesse, Claire and I are dating. I don't think it's any of your business but we haven't had sex…yet. I don't intend to hurt her, I care for her."

"Just so you understand, she is fragile and I'll be freaked out if you hurt her."

"Are you projecting your behavior onto me? That's a laugh. How many chicks have you hurt the last year?"

"That has nothing to do with what we are discussing. Claire is my sister and therefore my responsibility."

"Okay. Hang loose. Don't get your panties in a twist." John smirked.

"Just so we dig each other," Jesse said as he walked away, down the gangplank and out the dock to his boat.

Where did Jesse get off lecturing him, John fumed. He'd been a very poor example of how to treat chicks fairly. He checked his feelings for Claire. He did care about her, a lot. He'd even been thinking about keeping her in his life, permanently. But it would be a hard gig for a girl who couldn't walk. He wouldn't commit to her unless he was sure. And he wasn't sure about her feelings, how deep they were for him. He only knew he felt peaceful with her. Especially when they were singing together. He'd found out she could sing. Guess she got the same genes Jesse had. One thing was definite; he wasn't going all the way with her until he was sure of himself.

⤔

Bartok came on the Van Damme looking for Howard. The first person he saw was Cass sitting on deck.

"Is Howard around?" Bartok asked.

"Sure. In the wheelhouse."

Bartok knocked on the door. "Howard," he called.

Howard came to the door with a joint in his hand. "Yeah, what's happening?"

"Come out a minute I need to speak to you."

He followed Bartok over to the deck chairs and they sat down. Lia came out and sat with them.

"The Napa County State Hospital facility called me because that's the phone number they had for you," Bartok said.

Howard looked more alert and handed the joint to Lia. "What'd they want?"

"Faye is gone, Howard. She committed suicide." Bartok put his hand on his friends arm as he delivered the news.

For a minute Howard was silent. "What? How could that happen?"

"Apparently she had been saving her sedatives and took them all at once. She went peacefully."

Howard could hardly believe what Bartok was telling him. "I can't see how she could do it in that facility," Howard said.

Lia put out the joint and went behind Howard. She started rubbing his shoulders. Bartok still had his hand on Howard's arm.

"It happened. They want you to come up there and sign something so they aren't libel for anything."

"Those fuckers," Howard said. "All they want to do is cover their asses."

"They were going to send a statement to the court that Faye was able to stand trial. She was told and probably took the only way out she knew," Bartok said. "I'm so sorry, friend. Anything I can do?"

Howard shook his head.

"Give me a holler if you need anything." Bartok took his leave and went back to his boat.

Cass stood and went to Howard, taking his hand. Howard sat for a minute quietly and then he began to cry. His whole body shook as he sobbed. Lia tried to hold him by the shoulders but he was too big for her to get her arms around him.

"Come in the coffee house, Howard." She called as she headed for the galley. Howard stood and followed her, wiping his eyes.

Just then, Howie and Nancy came charging out of their room, having woken up from their naps.

"Daddy, Lia," they said simultaneously.

Cass intercepted them. "Hi. Daddy and Lia are busy right now, but I'm here. Want to go down to the dock for a while and look at the boats?"

Howie immediately said, "Yes, yes," but Nancy looked doubtful.

"Come on Nancy. When we get back I'll play paper dolls with you."

That convinced Nancy. "Okay."

Cass turned them toward the gangplank as she could still hear Howard sobbing. The three of them went out on the dock; Cass picked up Nancy and grabbed Howie's hand as they went slowly down the dock admiring the boats.

ᶜᵔ

The drive up to Napa County Hospital was quiet; Howard didn't say much. Lia was driving her MG. The sun was shining and the weather was lovely in Napa County. An eagle flew over them quite low. Lia thought this might be a good omen.

Once at the hospital, Howard was taken right into an office. He signed the paper that stated he wouldn't sue the Napa County State hospital for neglect. The administrator gave him a copy and he and Lia split the scene as quickly as possible.

He had taken a last look at Faye. Seemed they needed him to sign a paper that it was truly her. She looked as if she was peacefully sleeping. No marks on her, no bruising. He gave the facility a clean score.

He listened to the shrink, Dr. Lambert who told him in her opinion; Faye was ready to stand trial. Showed how much they knew about people. He told the shrink so, too.

Lia waited for him in the lobby. When he joined her she noticed the puffiness around his eyes was going away. His nose had regained its normal color.

"Did it bum you out, having to look at her?" she asked.

"No, it was all right."

"I'm shocked they kept her for a day and didn't send her to the morgue."

"They needed me to identify her."

"Now is she on her way to the morgue?"

Howard nodded.

"I'm so sorry, babe. But there was nothing you could have done." Lia held his hand.

"I know. It's just sad that the mother of my children is gone. I can't help feeling guilty."

"Yes, I know."

"I can't tell the kids. What should I do?"

Lia thought a minute. "I think you should wait until they are older. If they ask where their mother is, just say she's is sick and in the hospital."

Howard nodded. "I guess so."

They drove leisurely back to Sausalito, stopping at a little café in Petaluma. They drank an espresso and admired the little town with its hippie population and open air markets.

Back in the car, Howard brought up the children again. "What do you think I'll do with two kids to raise?"

Lia was slow to answer. "I guess you'll do the best you can."

"I plan on getting a job in September, but what will I do with them then?" Howard sounded anxious.

"I think you should look for a daycare and take them there while you're at work."

"Yeah, that's a cool idea. You'll be in school. Maybe we can make it work." Howard's agitation seemed to evaporate.

∽

Claire stood beside the picnic table on deck without holding on. "Look, John. I can stand alone."

John was overjoyed. "Good work, baby. Can you walk to me?"

"Not without my walker." She took hold of the walker and started toward John who was seated in a deck chair. She covered maybe ten feet and collapsed on the chair in John's arms.

"Wow, I'm really proud of you." He kissed her long and passionately. She returned his kiss.

"John, let's go to my room. I want to show you something."

Claire walked with the walker to her room down the deck toward the bow, a good twenty-five feet. John opened the door, picked her up with one arm and the walker with the other and kicked the door shut.

"What'd you want to show me?" he said, looking into her eyes.

"This." Claire put both her arms around his neck and kissed him. He placed her on the bunk bed and sat down beside her. Claire was unbuttoning her blouse.

"Are you sure you want to do this?" John asked.

Claire nodded as she slipped off her skirt. John looked at her lovely body, at her misshapen legs, at her intense face and eyes, and began undressing. They lay down together on the narrow bed.

⬲

Everyone on the Van Damme was sad about Faye's death. Friends of Howard's were especially sweet and kind to Howie and Nancy. Bartok offered to take care of the kids one night so Howard and Lia could have an evening out. Cass and Jesse went with them. They started out at Valhalla's for dinner, then walked to The Tides Book Store and had a coffee while perusing the books, then went to the nine-o'clock film, *Casablanca*, at the Gates Theater. After the film, they stopped at the No Name Bar for a drink. Howard drank beer, Lia and Cass drank wine, and Jesse drank Margaritas. Fortunately, Lia was the most sober and drove them back to the Van Damme in Howard's van. They were singing one of Jesse's songs, *Together Again*, as they clomped up the gangplank.

Bartok and Claire met them on deck. "Wow, you dudes are loud. Don't wake up the kiddies," he scolded.

The four of them hushed, remembering the kids.

"Howie and Nancy fell asleep while John and Spence were jamming in the coffee house. I put them to bed and nary a peep out of them," Bartok reported. "See you tomorrow," he said as he walked off the Van Damme.

"Thanks, Bartok," Howard called. Bartok waved.

Lia checked to see if the kids' room was locked and then she and Howard disappeared into the wheel house. Jesse and Cass went to her room.

"I got another gig for us next week in the city. It's a club called The Drinking Gourd. It should be a good place; We Five have played there as well as Red Legs. The Desperados will get a headline on their marquee." Jesse was excited.

"Sounds like fun," Cass said.

"We need to practice the new songs for that gig. Think you're up to singing them?"

Cass looked at Jesse. "Off course, why wouldn't I be?"

"You haven't been practicing with us lately. I wasn't sure why."

"I felt off the music, a little. I'm okay now."

"We'll have a rehearsal tomorrow on my boat. Okay?"

"Okay," Cass agreed.

"I'm gonna' go down to my boat and feed Kayak."

Cass nodded. "Are you coming back?"

"Probably not. I'll just climb into bed there." He

pulled her into an embrace and kissed her.

Cass wondered why he didn't want to walk the short distance back and spend the night with her. But she wasn't entirely unhappy about it. Jesse had been getting on her nerves lately.

～

John jumped onto Jesse's boat and stepped down into the cabin. Jesse was smoking a joint and picking his guitar.

"Jesse, I got some great news. Claire can sing! And she is walking a little with her walker. I was thinking we should let her sing with us on stage along with Cass. What do you think?"

Jesse was surprised. "She can sing? Does she know any of my songs?"

"Yup, she's picked them up during our sessions in The Ark. She is a quick learner, knows all the words and the music to most of our stuff."

"Sounds good but we can't have her walking onstage with her walker," Jesse said.

"I'll carry her on and set her in a chair. We can do it behind the curtain. The audience won't even know she uses a walker."

"We have the gig coming up next weekend at the Drinking Gourd. Is she ready?"

John nodded.

"Okay. Bring her to rehearsal tomorrow. We'll see what she can do."

"That will be a nice compliment for Cass. Can she sing harmony to Cass's melody?"

John nodded again. "She can sing anything. I swear she has the same genes as you."

John was so elated he scrambled off Jesse's boat and headed to the Van Damme to tell Claire the news.

24

*T*he ride over the Golden Gate Bridge was lovely; the stars were out on this particularly clear night. The moon shone its glorious light on San Francisco.

"The beginning of a great Friday night," Jesse said.

The Drinking Gourd was on Grant Street in North Beach, the hippest place to be in the city. All of the new bands and a few folk singers like Pete Seeger and Malvina Reynolds sang there.

The Desperados unpacked Howard's van and set up their instruments and equipment on the small stage. Cass helped Claire out of the van and inside the club.

By nine o'clock the place was crowded with standing room only. The band was crammed in the only dressing room backstage.

"There isn't a curtain. How are we going to get Claire onstage without anyone seeing?" asked Jesse.

"I think if you and I each take an arm and support her she can walk to the chair she will sit in," said John.

Jesse looked doubtful but nodded.

At nine-thirty sharp the manager gave the signal to start and the band had already tuned up.

Claire was seated by a mike and Cass stood beside her with her own mike. Jesse did a sound check and glanced at his band for readiness. He got a thumbs up.

The group broke into his latest song, *Together Again*, and the melody floated on the air currents across the club. Cass and Claire harmonized on the chorus and the guys sang the verses. The audience loved the song and broke into applause when Jesse finished the last lick on his guitar. The rest of the night was equally exciting for the listeners and by midnight with one break, the band finished off their gig with, *Napa County Circus Blues*.

On the way home, Claire fell asleep in the back of the van. "She isn't used to staying up so late," Cass told the guys.

Jesse was elated at their first night at The Drinking Gourd. "You and Claire did great, babe. We'll practice again tomorrow afternoon."

"Claire needs to get her sleep, Jesse," Cass said. "Don't make practice too early."

After they pulled into the Gate Six parking lot Jesse helped John get Claire into her room and Cass helped her get ready for bed.

Cass looked at Jesse. "Are you staying with me tonight?"

Jesse looked away. "I'm going on my boat to feed Kayak. I'll probably just stay there tonight."

As Cass walked to her room she wondered what was up with Jesse. That was the second night in a row he stayed on his boat and not with her. But she refused to let it bother her. He was a free entity, same as she was, and they both needed their alone time.

Jesse knew he was walking a fine edge and flirting with losing Cass if she ever found out. This cute little chick that had been stalking him at their last two gigs found her way onto his boat. Last night she was waiting for him and said she'd be back tonight. He just couldn't say no to her but he had to have her off the boat by tomorrow's practice. Otherwise he'd be in deep shit. Cass might not forgive him again. Oh well, weren't rock musicians supposed to have groupies hang around for sex and drugs? All the guys in the other bands had their groupies besides their old ladies. But Cass wasn't very understanding about it. In fact, he knew she never would be which didn't make for a lasting relationship with her in his mind. He'd just have to see where the future took him.

↩

Claire was humming one of Jesse's songs as she dressed. She knew all of his songs by heart now and harmonizing with Cass was so easy. It came to her naturally. Last night was such a wonderful experience. She had such a good time.

John had just left Claire's room. She knew she was falling in love with him. He was a tender lover and seemed to care a lot for her. Where their love affair was going, she didn't know or much care. She was living in the moment for the first time in her life. She was high on life and loving it.

She put on her new dress that Cass had helped her buy at the Salvation Army store. It was cotton and had large pockets in the skirt and a halter top. She felt very pretty in it; John had told her so. They were going to practice today on Jesse's boat and she hoped Jesse would let her sing one of his songs alone. Cass sung a couple of solos and Claire thought she was ready.

When she called her parents to tell them she was all right it was very traumatic for her. They wanted to know where she was and she wouldn't tell them; just that she was with Jesse. She figured that would make them worry less. The memories of the circus life were fading fast in Claire's mind. That life was over and gone, thank goodness.

She did her exercises and practiced with her walker going around and around her room. Her legs were getting stronger every day; she could feel the strength flowing through her muscles. One day she would walk with a cane; that was her goal.

She heard a knock. John opened the door and peeked in. When he saw she was up, he came in.

"Want to go to the deli for breakfast? Afterwards we'll go down to Jesse's for a practice session."

Claire nodded and grabbed her purse. John pulled her walker within reach and they made their way down the gangplank, John standing in front of the walker so it didn't get away from Claire. She walked all the way to the Deli with her walker, a feat for her.

They ordered omelets and toast. John touched Claire's arm.

"I need to tell you something. I just left Jesse on his boat and he has a young girl that stayed the night. I jumped all over him in front of her. She quickly dressed and left. Do you think I should tell Cass?"

Claire looked stunned. "Oh God, I don't know. It will hurt her terribly."

"I know, I know," John said. "But it's not fair to her."

"She may quit the band. She has before."

"Maybe I should hold off and see what happens. If Jesse straightens up, maybe I won't have to tell her. I really chewed him out and said what a dipshit he was to do this to Cass, so the girl knows he has a girlfriend."

"Maybe we should wait," Claire agreed.

Their food arrived and they started eating, but Claire was disturbed. "I don't want Cass to quit the band because without her I'm not as good."

"That's not true, honey. You have a lovely voice and you are a great addition to the group."

Claire flashed her usual sunny smile at John. "Thanks, darlin'."

⌇

By the time Claire and John arrived at Jesse's boat, Cass, David and Spence were already there and tuned up. John carried Claire down the cabin steps and placed her on the couch.

Jesse looked slightly guilty to Claire but nothing was said and Cass didn't seem to notice anything unusual.

"I've written a new tune so let's spend some time learning it this afternoon," Jesse said. "It's called *San*

Francisco Moonlight. It's kind of a love song." He looked at Cass and smiled. She smiled back.

Jesse handed out copies of the words and began playing the melody. "It's in the key of C, easy chording."

David who was the best guitarist in the band listened to the melody and immediately began experimenting with the melody, playing harmonies and grace notes along with Jesse.

"That's good, David," Jesse said excitedly. "Let's give the words a run-though."He looked pointedly at Claire and Cass. The girls picked up the melody quickly and in no time the band seemed to have the new song under control.

Jesse called a break, and Cass went back to the tiny head. She pulled the accordion door shut and lifted up the lid of the stool. As she sat down she glanced down at the waste basket and saw a wad of blonde hair resting on the top. She knew immediately it was recent and NOT Lia's who was the only blonde she knew. Cass picked up the hair and looked at it closely. It was several long strands. She threw them back in the basket, and sat on the stool with her head in her arms.

"Damn Jesse." She felt the tears pour down her cheeks. Why hadn't she listened to her gut instead of her heart? She knew he couldn't be faithful. All rock musicians were unfaithful. They called it being free… taking advantage of the opportunity of the moment. She didn't want a relationship with a man who was an overgrown teenager.

She sat on the covered stool and dried her tears. She placed the roll of hair in a piece of tissue and went back into the cabin. She walked up to Jesse and placed the hair on the knee of his jeans.

"I'm through with you and the band. Do not ever speak to me again." She turned and nearly stumbled over Claire's feet. Cass apologized and went up the steps of the cabin.

Jesse sat there silently and the rest of the guys looked away awkwardly. Claire began to cry and John got up to comfort her.

"Don't cry honey, it has nothing to do with you."

"But I love Cass and I want to sing with her in the band," Claire sobbed.

John shook his head and smoothed down her hair. "It's okay. Cass will have to work it out."

Jesse started retuning his guitar. "Let's do *Napa County Circus Blues*; we'll leave the new song for later."

David and Spence put up their instruments in their cases. "I think I've had all the entertainment I can stand for today," David said. "See ya' later." He and Spence left the cabin and Claire, Jesse and John heard them step out of the boat and onto the dock.

Cass cried all the way down the dock to the Van Damme. She went immediately to her room and pushed the trunk against the door, threw herself on her bunk and continued having a good cry.

She heard a knock and David said, "Cass, can I come in?"

"Not right now. Go away. I'll see you later."

Then there was silence and she continued to sob. What was she thinking that Jesse would change? He'd done this once before that she knew of and now it was apparent he needed to have many sexual partners. She was in denial, she knew. It was time to return to Los Angeles and get on with her life down there.

⁓

John helped Claire off the boat and Jesse sat alone in his cabin picking the guitar and thinking. What had he done wrong? He just wanted to live the life of freedom like all the other rock musicians did. If he saw a stone fox and wanted to score with her, why not? Cass was just not the woman for him. He needed an old lady that was hip and wouldn't get all flipped out because he had a one night stand. A woman that looked the other way would be cool for him. He would miss Cass though. She was a fine singer and a fine addition to the Desperados. Thank God he had Claire to sing along with the band. She was working out just fine.

Jesse lay down his 12-string and went up top with Kayak. The wind was down and the sun was warm on his face. The waves were slapping against the hull. He would definitely miss Cass but he could get along without her. He wouldn't sweat this breakup.

He settled down in a chair, closed his eyes and began thinking about a new song that was in his head. Faithful Kayak lay beside him on the deck.

Lia and Howard came out of the wheel house and Lia thought about checking on the kids who were taking a nap. It was about time for them to wake up and she needed to think about feeding them.

John and Claire were sitting on the deck, talking. Claire motioned them over.

"Cass found out about Jesse's latest one night stand and she quit the band and quit Jesse too," Claire said, between sighs.

Lia sat down with them. "What happened?"

"Cass found some hair in the waste basket on Jesse's boat and she just up and quit," John explained.

Howard shook his head. "I told Jesse he was playing a dangerous game. Cass wouldn't stand for it if she found out."

"Yeah, we all told him," Lia said.

"This is the second time Cass knows about and she isn't going to forgive him this time," Claire said. "And I don't blame her a bit."

"Thankfully we have Claire to sing with the band," John said, smiling at Claire.

"I don't much feel like singing without Cass."

"You'll be okay. You know all the songs."

Claire nodded, but looked sad.

"Where is Cass now?" Lia asked.

"Not sure," John answered. "Probably in her room."

25

*L*ife went on as usual on the Van Damme, the Desperados continued to play at the local clubs with Claire singing lead and Cass made preparations to leave and go back to Los Angeles. She told Lia she would take the bus home.

Lia and Cass were sitting on the deck having a brew. Howie and Nancy were playing on the floor of the deck. "Why don't you wait for a month then I'll drive back down to L.A.? I've decided to move up here and live with Howard. I've registered at UC Berkeley for my senior year. Before the semester starts I'll go down and get my stuff and bring it back."

"I don't want to have to talk to Jesse. I'm done with him."

Lia squeezed her beer can flat. "You can avoid him. Just don't come out in the evenings when he and the band are playing in the coffee house."

Cass nodded. "I'll think about it. I would like to spend a little more time with Claire before I leave."

"Good idea. She needs your friendship."

Cass looked at her friend. "So you've decided to be with Howard? I'm glad. You two make a good couple. Howard doesn't seem to have to score with the groupies." Cass looked out across the bay.

"Howard looks, but he doesn't act on his looking. That's the difference between him and Jesse. Jesse just hasn't grown up."

"Don't I know that," Cass agreed.

"I like Jesse a lot and he's a very talented musician, but he's not permanent partner material. He does not make for a good old man."

"We're history, so no need to talk about him anymore. I just don't want to waste my time."

"I understand. You'll meet someone eventually that will appreciate you. Just takes time."

Cass slipped out of the chair to the deck and started playing with Nancy and her paper dolls. Lia pulled Howie on her lap and began telling him a story.

⌐

It was a particularly beautiful morning at Waldo Point. The sun was shining, reflecting off the sparkling chrome on the houseboats. Sea gulls swooped across the decks and landed on riggings.

Bartok was running from his boat to the Van Damme as fast as his short legs would propel him.

He came rushing on deck yelling, "Howard, Howard…"

Howard burst out of the wheel house. "What's up?"

"Jesse's been arrested for possession of coke. He's in the Marin County jail. He just called and wants us to bail him out." Bartok was breathing heavily from his climb up the gangplank.

"What? How'd it happen?" Howard asked.

"He was stopped for speeding on the freeway. When they looked in the car, Jesse had an envelope of coke in plain sight. He says it was 8 grams. The cops arrested him on the spot and impounded his van."

"Jesus, what was he thinking?" Howard murmured.

"A coke arrest will be high bail, probably, around $50 K. I could put up half of 10%, $2500. Can you go the other half?"

"I can. Do we have a lawyer we can hire to represent him?"

"We could get Jay Goldstein, an old friend. He'd probably represent Jesse."

Howard shook his head. "Why the hell doesn't Jesse get his shit together? This is bad news for the band. Can you give the lawyer a call and see what he says?"

Bartok nodded. "I'll go back to my boat and call."

"Okay," Howard says.

Cass was standing at the top of the stairs. She heard the conversation with Bartok and Howard.

"Jesse is in jail?" she asked Howard.

Howard nodded. "Bartok and I will try to bail him out."

"It serves him right. Maybe this will give him more of a sense of responsibility," Cass said.

"He's going to get a jail sentence for this, Cass," Bartok said. "They've been busting people for coke and giving them a couple of years."

Cass looked dejected. She shouldn't care what happened to Jesse now, but in her heart she did.

"I'll contact the lawyer. This is Friday so Jesse will probably be in jail over the weekend. Get back to you, later." Bartok left the Van Damme.

Cass sat down with Howard. Lia came out of the wheel house and joined them. "I heard. Too bad for the band. Without Jesse and you singing, Cass, they will probably have to cancel their upcoming gigs."

"Probably," Cass agreed.

John came up top and asked what the noise was all about. Howard told him.

"Shit. Jesse got busted. That's great." John lit a joint and shook his head. "That may be a problem for the band. Without him or Cass singing, we have only Claire for vocals."

Claire came out of her room on the bow. "What's happening?"

Howard told her.

"Jesse got busted? Oh, no!" She started to cry.

John came over and comforted her. "Honey, nothing you can do about it. Bartok is hiring a lawyer right now. He and Howard are going to put up bail. But he won't get out of jail before Monday."

Claire continued to sob, and Cass handed her a tissue. "We just have to wait, honey," Cass said.

"I'm glad Howard cleaned up the boat when Howie and Nancy came here to live," Lia said. "No more dishes of drugs and acid Kool-aid sitting around. But, Howard, we need to get rid of the bong in the coffee house. You know the cops will be here and do a search."

"Yeah, okay." Howard went to the coffee house and brought back a large bong. "Where should I stash it? It won't fit in my dope stash under the wheel."

"How about taking it to Bartok's?" Lia suggested.

Howard agreed and immediately left the boat.

"The cops could arrive at any time," Lia said. "I suggest everyone put their drugs with ours under the wheel in the wheel house. It looks like a permanent structure and doesn't lift up easily." John went to his room and brought back his stash of marijuana.

"The authorities have been very lenient with us up until now. They have never raided the coffee house," John noted. "But I agree with Lia. They will be here now."

"Someone needs to go on Jesse's boat and clean out any dope," Lia said.

John volunteered. "I'll go. I know where he keeps his stash."

Howard returned and he and John headed for Jesse's boat. After taking Jesse's stash to Bartok's Howard returned and brought Kayak and some dog food on the Van Damme. Kayak was installed in Cass's room very quickly. She really loved the dog.

⌐

The very next day two uniformed cops pulled up in front of the Van Damme. They walked up the gangplank and saw Howard sitting in the sun. Kayak was lying beside him and growled when the two men stepped onto the deck.

Howard put his hand on Kayak's neck. "It's okay, boy. They are friends."

The cops approached slowly, not wanting to have a run in with Kayak, and introduced themselves.

"We have to search the boat because of Jesse Powers' arrest," the Lieutenant said.

"Jesse doesn't live on this boat. His boat is down the dock," Howard said.

"We know. We have a search warrant to go on his boat. We don't have one for the Van Damme, but we'd like your permission to do a search."

"I'm gonna let you search the boat anyway," Howard said. "'Cause I can tell you we have no drugs on board."

The police started below deck. They searched all the rooms, including Cass's. She was startled when the cop opened her door.

"Sorry miss, we are searching for drugs. Have to check your room."

"Go ahead," she said.

One officer looked under her mattress, in the desk drawers, under the seats of the chairs, and under her pillow. He picked up her guitar and shook it. Satisfied that nothing was hidden inside he put it down. When he had finished he smiled and left.

There was a loose board against the wall behind her bunk that she had found. He didn't see that. It was a large enough space she could stash drugs, but she hadn't.

When they had finished below deck they came up and started on the coffee house, then the kitchen. They checked the head, Claire's room and the wheel house. They found nothing. They didn't even give the old wooden wheel that used to propel the boat, a second glance.

"Thanks for making our job easier," the cop said. "We're headed down to Jesse's boat."

"No one there so you won't need the warrant," Howard said.

"Thanks for your cooperation," one of the cops said.

When they left Cass came up top. "Sure glad they didn't find anything. You guys scoured Jesse's boat?"

"Yeah, we found his stash but we took it over to Bartok's. We figured he wouldn't be searched."

"Bartok is taking a chance," Cass said.

"If they intended to search every house boat here then Bartok would probably be included, but we didn't think that was their goal."

"I'm going down when they leave to lock up Jesse's cabin," Howard said. "All his music equipment and guitars are in there and I'd hate to have them ripped off."

"You have a key?" Cass asked.

Howard nodded. "We all exchange keys. Bartok has keys to several house boats here in the harbor."

Lia woke up Nancy and Howie from the make-shift bed on deck and herded them into the coffee house to feed them some dinner.

"I'll come and help," Cass said. Kayak followed everyone into the kitchen.

John approached Cass on that Friday afternoon. "We need you to sing with our band tonight at the Drinking Gourd in the city. The club owner said no Jesse and no Cass equals no gig. He said if you and Claire sing we have a job."

Cass thought about it. "Okay. I'll sing tonight and tomorrow night, but when Jesse's back I'm out of here."

"Thanks, babe," John said and gave her a hug.

That evening they packed up Howard's van and headed for the Drinking Gourd. The place was crowded and the band gave it their best, but Cass's heart was not into singing. She missed having Jesse to relate to. She tried relating with Claire but she was not into it either. The band played like they had a musician missing. But the crowd seemed not to notice. After three hours of music, the band packed up and drove home.

Cass fell into bed, Kayak beside her on the floor.

The Saturday night performance was the same. No one had their hearts into it. Jesse was missing and he was the band.

26

Jesse stayed in jail for the weekend. Jay Goldstein represented him in court on Monday morning. His bail was $50,000 of which Bartok and Howard paid the 10% bail money. Bartok and Howard were there to take him home.

"Thanks for getting me out," Jesse said to Bartok and Howard, squeezing their shoulders.

Jesse looked haggard and dirty. He'd slept in his clothes and hadn't even had an opportunity to wash up.

Jay, his lawyer was charging him $2000 to represent him. Jesse said he would give him a check back on his boat.

They drove back to the Van Damme where Claire and Kayak were waiting.

When Kayak saw Jesse he bounded forward. Jesse bent down and Kayak licked his face.

"I missed you, boy," Jesse said as he hugged Kayak.

Claire walked over with her walker and hugged her brother. "You better be more careful from now on. I worried about you."

Jesse nodded sheepishly. "Thanks for keeping Kayak and feeding him," he said to Claire.

"It wasn't me, it was Cass. He stayed in her room."

Just then, Cass came up on deck.

Jesse turned to her. "Thanks for keeping Kayak."

"Of course," she said.

He turned to Howard and Bartok. "I need to play a few more gigs before I can repay you. Is that ok?"

"Sure, no hurry," Bartok said. Howard agreed.

"We took your stash over to Bartok's before the cops searched your boat," Howard said.

"Thanks for that," Jesse said. "Guess I have a lot of good friends here. I'm very grateful."

Howard produced a key. "I locked up the cabin so the music equipment was safe."

Jesse nodded and thanked Howard again.

"I'll walk with you and head over to my boat and get your stuff," Bartok offered.

Jesse looked around at Claire and Cass. "Thanks for everything."

"Can I come over later," Claire asked.

"Sure. Just let me get a few hours nap. How'd the gig go Friday and Saturday?"

Claire told him they wouldn't give them the gig unless Cass sang, too. "We didn't have our hearts in it with you gone, Jesse," Claire said.

Jesse nodded again and looked at Cass. "See you all, later."

27

The next day Jesse called a practice session on his boat. John picked up Claire. Spence and David showed up. They were practicing some of Jesse's new songs.

"Stop," Jesse held up his hand. "Claire you have to come in stronger. You don't have Cass's strong voice to follow. You have to do it yourself."

Claire began to tear up and John put down his guitar. "Come on, Jesse. Be cool. She's doing her best."

Jesse rubbed the back of his neck. "I know, I'm sorry, Sis. Just try to sing louder. Let's start from the top."

They sang one of Jesse's newest tunes, *Jesse's Song*. Claire hadn't learned it all as she didn't have Cass to help her memorize the words. She mumbled through part of it and hummed with her lovely contralto voice.

Jesse stopped playing. "You have to learn the words, Claire. Humming doesn't do it."

"I will, Jesse. I haven't had Cass to help me memorize them."

"I'll help her," John said. "After practice we'll sit down and do it, okay?" He looked at Claire.

"Okay." Claire's lips were trembling.

"Let's leave this song and go with an old one. Jesse started, *Napa County Circus Blues* and everyone joined in.

After the practice John took Claire back to the Van Damme. They sat down on deck and went over the words to the new song. Lia and Howard were still on deck playing with Nancy with Howie.

"Where is Cass," John asked.

"She walked downtown to the Tides Book Store," Lia said.

"I'd really like her to help Claire learn the words to this new song of Jesse's. Know when she'll be back?"

Lia shook her head. "Probably around dinner time. She usually helps me then." Lia looked at John and Claire. "You really need to realize Cass is not invested in the band anymore. She may not want to help Claire."

"I understand where she's coming from, but she means no ill will toward the band. If she can help Claire I'll bet she'll do it."

Lia shrugged. "Maybe. We'll see."

⌐

Cass returned from downtown Sausalito around five o'clock. When she walked on deck of the Van Damme she heard John and Claire practicing a song.

Claire called to her. "Cass, could you come over here, please?"

She walked over to them and sat down at the picnic table. "What's up?"

"We were wondering if you would help Claire with Jesse's new song," John asked. "She hasn't quite got the hang of the melody and the words."

"Sure," Cass answered.

"Out of sight, Cass," Claire said in a relieved manner.

"I'll help you here but I won't go on Jesse's boat during practice."

"Okay," Claire said.

Just as John was handing the guitar to Cass, they could hear a vehicle pull up below the gangplank in the parking lot. Cass got up to take a look. A VW van with tie-dyed curtains and 'San Francisco or Bust,' and 'Acid Kool-aid,' written on the side of the van had parked right beside the Van Damme boat. Black smoke billowed from the exhaust pipe as the vehicle came to rest. Music blared from inside; The Beach Boys, *Surfin'*, bit the air like a hot summer day. Six people tumbled out of the van; a couple of chicks and four dudes.

Cass recognized the guy getting out of the driver's side; her old singing buddy and ex-boyfriend, Tony Grieva. Tony looked around at the harbor and then spied Cass on deck.

He waved. "Hey, foxy lady. How's the atmosphere up there?"

"Fine. What are you doing in this part of the country?"

"I heard about The Ark and me and the band thought we'd come up and check it out."

"Come aboard," Cass called down.

She turned to Claire and John. By this time, Lia and Howard were on deck too. "Some guys I know in Los Angeles came up to play at The Ark."

Howard went to the side and watched the guys unload sleeping bags, suitcases, instruments and bags of food.

"Looks like we'll have a jam session tonight," Howard said, smiling. "They brought food too, how thoughtful."

Six people trudged up the gangplank, arms full. Tony set down his load and grabbed Cass in a bear hug. "How's my favorite fox?" he said, looking closely at Cass.

"I'm good."

Cass turned and introduced the band to everyone. There was Bill, Phillip, Casey and Tony. The two girls were new to Cass. "They call themselves the Sunny Day Band. I used to sing with them occasionally," Cass said.

"These two chicks are Linda and Brenda, our back-up singers," Tony said.

The rest of the band set down their loads. Howard fired up a bong and passed it around.

"Cool," John said. "Tonight we'll have a great jam session in the coffee house."

"How'd you hear about The Ark in Los Angeles?" Howard asked.

"Man, everybody connected to the music scene knows about Sausalito and The Ark," Tony said. He hadn't taken his eyes off Cass. She smiled at him and he smiled back.

"Didn't realize our reputation reached that far away," Howard mused. "That's cool."

The bong had made its way around the group and needed replenishing.

"Lia, honey, take everyone below deck and show them where they can bunk," Howard instructed.

The Sunny Day Band picked up their various belongings and followed Lia below deck.

"So what's the story with you and Tony?" Howard inquired, eyebrows lifted.

Cass moved over beside him. "We were together a while ago after I split up with Jack. We remained friends."

"I saw the way he looked at you. If you were a cookie he'd eaten you up."

Cass and Howard laughed out loud. "Yeah, I noticed," Cass said.

"I sang with their band for a while and we got together. When I left to come up here I told him we were over."

"It doesn't look like it's over for him," Howard said.

"Maybe not," Cass agreed.

Lia came back on deck with Tony. He walked over to Cass and sat down beside her.

"I didn't know you were here. I just want you to know I wasn't stalking you." He laughed as he lit a joint.

"I know, Tony. It's cool."

"Glad you and your band came up. We have some good jamming here evenings. A lot of the Bay Area musicians come here to The Ark," Howard said.

"I'm looking forward to it. Thanks for the opportunity, Howard," Tony said.

Bartok came on deck and was introduced to Tony. The rest of the band filtered up on deck with their instruments and sat in the sun. Soon the deck was awash with great music. Bill played bongos, Casey mandolin and guitar and Tony on Guitar. The music wafted over Waldo Point like a wave. Before long Jesse came over to the Van Damme and sat down listening to the new band. Dave and Spence came up from below deck with their instruments and the entire deck was throbbing with music.

After an hour the musicians took a break. Jesse introduced himself and got introduced to the Sunny Day Band.

"Wow that was some bitchin' music. Real surfin' sounds," Jesse said.

"Yeah, we are heavily influenced by The Beach Boys," Tony said.

Tony went over to Cass. "Care to show me the marina?"

Cass hesitated, then, "Sure." She jumped up and she and Tony went down the gangplank.

Jesse watched. "Who are these guys and how come Cass knows them?" he asked Howard.

Howard explained that Cass used to sing with them in L.A. but he didn't mention that Tony and Cass had once been a couple.

Jesse hung around talking to the band and waiting for Cass to return. When she and Tony came back from their walk they got into Tony's van and took off. Jesse returned to his boat.

⌒

"Where are we going?" Tony asked.

"We're headed to downtown Sausalito." When they got to the Tides Book Store Cass pointed out the parking lot across the street. Tony parked and they got out and walked.

"Let's go to the book store. Are you hungry? We could have lunch," Cass suggested.

"Okay," Tony replied.

They entered the book store and found seats in the café. Cass ordered a tuna sandwich and Tony ordered a hamburger and coffee for both of them.

"So tell me, why are you up here and why have you stayed so long?"

"I came up with Lia whose boyfriend Howard runs the boat. The life on the Van Damme is fun and never a dull minute. I've been singing with Jesse's band, The Desperados, at gigs around San Francisco." Cass took a deep breath. She didn't need to say too much.

"Why did you leave me and L.A.?" he asked.

"I just needed to get away. Lia offered this opportunity and I took it."

Tony took a drink of his coffee. "I've really missed you, Cass." He covered her hand with his.

She left her hand where it was. "I missed you too, Tony. But I've been so busy learning new songs, helping Lia and Howard on the boat. I haven't wanted to leave here."

"Can we pick up where we left off?" Tony asked, looking into her eyes.

"I don't think so, Tony. We can be friends, though."

He removed his hand. "Have you fallen for one of the guys up here?"

Cass shook her head vehemently. "Absolutely not. I'm just enjoying being a free entity again."

"I care about you. I want you for my old lady." Tony continued to press his case.

"I care about you too, but I've seen how the group-ies hang around the musicians here and I don't want to be any part of it."

"Did I ever give you a reason to think I swapped spit with any of the chicks that hung around our band?"

"No you didn't. I just don't want to be hooked up with a musician."

Tony hung his head and nodded. "I dig," he said, sadly.

They finished their lunch, Tony paid the bill and they continued to walk around Sausalito. Tony did seem impressed with the beauty of the harbor; the fine summer day, the sun shining above them, causing Cass to squint when she looked at the Golden Gate Bridge before they got back in Tony's van and returned to the Van Damme.

⌒

When Tony and Cass went on deck, Lia was feeding Howie and Nancy dinner at the picnic table. Howard had rolled a few joints and left them on the table. The

Sunny Day Band was sprawled around in the deck chairs napping or smoking.

Claire and John were missing. So were Jesse and David and Spence.

"The guys and Claire are over on Jesse's boat practicing," Howard offered the information unasked.

Cass ignored the remark. "Hey, I'd like to hear them play. Think we could go over there?" Tony asked.

Cass shook her head. "They don't like listeners when they're not performing."

Tony shrugged his shoulders. "I'm going to go down below and take a nap. We found a room with four bunks. The girls have another room across the hall."

"Cool," Cass said.

"See you later," he said.

When he was gone, Lia and Howard wanted to know where they went. Cass told them.

"I'm making lasagna for dinner, Cass," Lia said. "Will you help?"

"Of course."

"With the extra people we need to make six large pans. Think that will be enough?"

"If it isn't, they'll just have to eat pie." The Sunny Day Band had brought five apples pies that they had picked up at a local bakery.

Lia and Cass headed for the kitchen to prepare the evening meal.

⌐

Jesse came on to the deck of the Van Damme with his guitar and Kayak. Music poured from the coffee house; as people danced to the surfing sounds of The Sunny Day Band.

He spotted Cass on stage singing with the group. She held the mike so Tony could sing into it. She was singing harmony to his main melody. They were turned toward each other and singing to each other.

Jesse sat down at one of the front tables, Kayak by his chair. He was not happy seeing Cass sing with this group. He knew it was her old band, but he still didn't like it.

When they finished the surfin' song they walked off stage. John, David and Spence came on and started setting up their instruments and sound. Jesse climbed on stage and began tuning up. John helped Claire on stage into a comfortable chair.

"What'd you think about their sound?" John whispered in Jesse's ear.

"Sounds like they're imitating The Beach Boys," he said.

John nodded, agreeing.

"Did you learn the words to the new song," he asked Claire.

She nodded.

The Desperados tuned up and opened with their new song, *Early Morning Music*. The beginning was weak and Claire didn't come in when she should have. Jesse stopped playing. So did everyone else. "Let's take it again, from the top," he said crossly.

They started the song again and Cass came up front to coach Claire when to come in with the vocals. Claire came in on time and Cass went back to sit with Tony and the group. Linda and Brenda, the back-up singers had come up from below deck.

"I used to sing with this band until just recently," Cass explained to Tony.

"Why'd you stop singing?" Tony asked.

"I quit the group. Internal problems," she said.

"What problems," Tony asked.

"I don't want to talk about it, okay?"

Tony shrugged. "Okay."

Cass stayed until the band had finished their set. Other musicians joined them on stage and soon there was hardly any walking room.

"You're welcome to go up and jam with them," Cass said to her friends.

"We'll just stay back here. We really don't play their kind of music," Tony said.

Cass left the group and went out on deck. Lia and Howard and Bartok were sitting at the picnic table sharing a joint. Bartok passed it to Cass.

"Nice music coming from inside. I think Claire's fittin' in real good with the Desperados," Bartok reflected.

"She needs some more practice with the new song, but yes, she is doing fine," Cass said.

"I liked the surfing music your old band played. You sounded mighty fine singing with them," Bartok said.

"Thanks, dear," Cass said and kissed the top of his head.

"Did Jesse say anything to you?" Lia asked.

"Nope."

"Are you not speaking?"

"Not really. I have nothing to say to him."

They finished the joint and the four of them went into the coffee house to listen to the music. A couple of musicians from Red Legs showed up and were jamming on their guitars. Jesse was right with them, as was John, Spence and David.

Claire had gone off stage and was down at a front table. Lia, Cass, Howard and Bartok sat with her and Howard brought out the bong. Howie and Nancy were fast asleep; the evening meal was cleaned up and the music went on far into the wee hours of the morning.

28

*I*t was early, not yet 8 a.m. The seagulls were singing across Waldo Point, the sun was just coming out from behind a fluffy cloud. Jesse bounded up the Van Damme gangplank and saw that Cass was not on deck. He ran down below and knocked at Cass's door.

"Who is it," Cass called out.

"Jesse."

"Go away. I don't want to talk to you."

"Please Cass, I need your help. Would you just come to the door?"

A minute later, Cass opened the door. "What?" she said.

"Could I come in? I need to talk a bit to you."

"You can talk right there. What's up?"

Jesse stood with his arm resting on the door jam. "I need to sell some songs so I can pay back Howard. He needs the money before Bartok does. I want you to negotiate with Paul to buy about 10 of my songs."

Cass looked at Jesse. "You can do it. Just tell him how much bread you want for them and make sure he gives you a written contact."

"I would feel better if you did the negotiating. I need to get $2400 for the ten songs. Do you think he will go for that?"

Cass shook her head and looked down. "I don't know." She looked up at him. "But we sure will give it

194

a sailor's try." She smiled.

"Oh, thanks, babe. I really appreciate this."

"I'm not doing it for you, Jesse. I'm doing it for Howard. Go call Paul and have him come over here. We are not going there."

"Bitchin'. I'll go over to Bartok's right now and call him." Jesse turned and ran up the stairs to the deck.

Cass grabbed her sweater and followed him on deck.

Ten minutes later Jesse was back on the Van Damme deck. "Paul said he'd be here tomorrow afternoon. I told him I wanted to sell a few songs. Didn't say how many."

"I'll try to get $2400 for them, Jesse, but I can't guarantee he'll go for it. Do you know which songs you want to sell?"

"Yeah, all of my new ones. I have about seven new ones. And I have three in my repertoire that the band plays."

"I hope you know what you're doing. You are essentially giving away your creative talents to Paul."

"I know, but Howard needs the cash to live on. I can't make enough playing gigs in the city to pay him back quickly. He has to feed his kids and keep the coffee house going."

Cass nodded and started thinking how she would sweet-talk Paul into accepting the deal she had in mind.

⌐

The next afternoon Paul Zanes drove up in his 1940 Rolls and parked beside the Van Damme gangplank.

He labored up the plank and saw Jesse and Cass sitting at the picnic table.

"Hello my lovely lady," he said to Cass, then nodded to Jesse.

"Paul let's get right down to business. Jesse wants to sell 10 of his songs; seven of them are brand new. He needs to get $2800 for them, and that's the deal. They will be worth a fortune when your main singers record them, so you are set to make a lot of bread."

Paul laughed his big guffaw. "I don't think The Beach Boys ten songs are worth $2800."

Jesse bristled at this comment but remained quiet.

"Regardless, we're offering them to you first. And The Desperados will have the right to play and sing these songs even after your people have recorded them."

"I don't think so," Paul said, shaking his head. "How about "$1900 for the ten songs."

Cass was silent a moment. "We'll take $2500 for the ten songs and that's final. I should let you know that Bill Graham is coming tomorrow to negotiate for the songs. So if you don't pick them up, he will."

Paul wiped the smile off his face. "Graham is coming?"

Cass nodded.

Paul was silent for a few minutes. Cass put her hand over Jesse's hand on the bench to keep him quiet.

Finally Paul spoke. "$2500 for ten songs! I want the words and music to all ten. No need to record them, Jesse."

Cass pulled two pieces of paper from a folder in front of her. "Here's a contract for you to sign." She slid it over to Paul.

"What!" Paul squawked. "Another contract? What's wrong with the one I signed before?"

"Nothing except that was for that group of songs. This is for these ten songs."

Paul read over the document then took up the pen on the table and signed both copies. Cass pushed one over to Paul and put the other one in the folder. He pulled out a checkbook. "Okay if I give you a check, Jesse?"

Jesse looked at Cass and she nodded. "Sure," he said.

Paul wrote out a check for $2500 and slid it over to Cass. She handed it to Jesse. "It's been fine doing business with you, Paul." Cass stood and offered her hand.

Paul looked at her hand and thought a minute, then he shook it. "You drive a hard bargain, lady."

"Thanks," Cass replied. She headed for the galley.

"Come with me to my boat and I'll give you the music," Jesse said. He and Paul left the Van Damme. Cass watched them go from inside the coffee house.

Lia and Howard came up behind her. They had been in the galley. "We heard you and Paul. Man, you managed a bitchin' agreement," Howard said.

"That was pretty cool the way you threatened him with Bill Graham. Is he really coming tomorrow?" Lia asked.

Cass smiled. "Nope, but I think I did a cool bluff. Paul fell for it." Cass went to the cooler and pulled out a beer. "I only did it because Jesse said the bread was to pay you back for the bail money you loaned him."

"Thanks, Cass," Howard said as he put his arm around her and hugged her.

Lia hugged them both in a three-way embrace. "Try not to be too hard on Jesse. You know he's still a little boy in a lot of ways," Lia said.

"I just don't want to be friends with him. I'm still hurt and I won't let him get close to me again."

"We dig that," Howard said.

"I got to get the kiddies up from their nap. Time to feed them dinner," Lia said. "Are you going to be around at dinner time, Cass?" Lately Cass had been walking down to the Tides for dinner.

"Probably, why?"

"We have six more mouths to feed with the Sunny Day Band and a couple more musicians coming from the city. Could you help me with the meal?"

"Of course. What are you planning?"

"I have two pots of spaghetti sauce simmering. I thought we'd cook up a bunch of pasta and rice and serve some veggie sticks and dip. When we run out of pasta we can put the sauce on rice."

"Okay. Let's get started," Cass soaped her hands and rinsed them by pouring water from a pitcher. Water was important to conserve on the boat as they had no water hook-ups to the city. She put a small amount of pasta in some boiling water for Howie and Nancy.

Lia came back with the kids and sat them down at a table in the coffee house. Cass put two plates of spaghetti sauce and pasta in front of them. Then she and Lia began the evening preparations.

29

$\mathcal{A}$t dinner Jesse was telling the group at the table which included the guys from the Sunny Day Band how cool Cass pulled off the deal that afternoon with Paul Zanes, one of the leading record producers in the Bay Area.

"Hey, maybe we need you for our business manager," Tony said. He was sitting beside Cass and he put his hand on her shoulder.

"I'm no one's business manager," she said. "I helped Jesse out because he owed Howard for the bread to get him out of jail."

"Hey, man, what were you in jail for," Tony asked.

"Cocaine. Just a small amount, but bail was five grand."

One guy in the other band rolled his eyes. Everyone laughed like it was funny.

"If it wasn't for Howard and Bartok I'd still be in jail, freaking out," Jesse said.

"Outta sight, man," Tony said. "You're lucky you have a friend like Cass, too."

Jesse looked at Cass but she wouldn't meet his eyes.

"You got that right," Jesse said.

When everyone had finished, Lia and Cass picked up the dishes and brought out the banana bread.

"Far Out," Tony said. "Do you eat like this every night?"

"Yup," Lia said.

"I could get used to this," Tony said.

"Sure glad you guys dropped by for a few days to experience The Ark and the Van Damme. Do you know when you'll be leaving?" Howard asked.

Tony stopped laughing and the rest of the guys sobered. "Uh...probably in a few more days. Do you have a time you want us to leave?"

"A couple of days would be fine," Howard said.

"Sure," Tony said. The guys in the band began collecting their instruments and took them back below deck.

When they had all gone Jesse turned to Howard. "How come you kicked them off the boat so soon?"

"I just thought we don't need Cass tempted by other bands."

"I get your drift," Jesse said, smiling.

All six of members of the Sunny Day Band came back on deck. "Think we'll take a run downtown. Anyone want a lift?" Tony asked.

No one answered so the four guys and two girls went down the gangplank and got in their van.

⌐

Later that night the Southern California Band came back to the boat and took seats in the coffee house. When Cass finished a solo set, the band got onstage and did a set of their surfin' songs. After five songs, Tony spoke into the mike: "This will be our last night here in Sausalito. We've really enjoyed The Ark experience and thanks to Howard for the opportunity. Thanks to all the people in the audience for listening."

Tony and the group played another surfing song and got a healthy applause. They packed up their instruments and sound equipment and carried everything down to their van.

Tony went to sit with Cass at a front table. "How come you guys are splitting?" Cass asked.

"We just thought it was time. Don't want to wear out our welcome."

"Hey, did someone make you feel unwanted?" Cass asked.

"Nope, just thought it was time we got back to L.A." Tony lit up a joint. "Cass, would you consider coming back with us? Joining our band again? We really would love to have you with us, again? I'd really like you to be my old lady, too."

Cass was surprised at Tony suggestion. "Uh…I don't think so right now. I am coming back to L.A. soon. Lia has to go back to get her things; she's moving up here with Howard. I still have an apartment I'm making rent payments on."

"You mean you're coming back to stay in L.A.?" Tony asked.

She nodded. "I only intended to be here for the summer."

"Do you think we might get back together then?" Tony took her hand.

"We'll see. Okay?" She pulled her hand from Tony's. "But I'll get in touch with you when I get back."

Tony leaned over and kissed her on the lips. Cass didn't pull away. "I'll see you in the morning before we leave." He said. He was leaning into her shoulder when Jesse came into the coffee house and saw them.

He made a beeline for Tony and Cass. "What's goin' on here?" Jesse growled.

Cass looked up. "Nothing, Jesse. This isn't any of your business so back off."

"Cass is my woman and I want you out of here," Jesse said to Tony.

"Wait a minute. I'm no one's woman, least of all yours."

Tony had stood up and was standing nose to nose with Jesse.

Howard moved in. "Okay, guys. This is a no-win situation. Cass is her own boss. No one has any rights on her."

Jesse unclenched his fists. Tony took a step backwards.

"I'm glad everyone digs this," Cass said. "No reason for anyone to get upset. Tony was saying goodbye as he and the band are leaving in the morning."

"Let's all hang loose," Howard said. Tony smiled at Cass and went below deck. Jesse sat down beside her at the table.

"I'm sorry I got riled," he said.

"I never would have pegged you for jealous," Cass said grinning.

"Me either," he said sheepishly. "I saw him kissing you and my mind freaked out."

"We're good friends, and he is leaving in the morning."

"Were you his chick in L.A.?"

Cass nodded, "A long time ago. Since then we've been friends." She thought a little lie to Jesse would be the best answer.

"I'm glad he's leaving. Any chance you'll sing with us again? Maybe here, tonight?"

"No Jesse. I'm not getting involved in your band again or with you. Let's just leave it at that."

"I've apologized to you and I'll do anything to get you back. I'm crazy about you, babe." He put his arm around her shoulder.

Cass stood. "No Jesse. You hurt me and I won't let myself in for any more hurt."

Jesse dropped his arm. Cass looked into his eyes. She saw desire and trouble. "Let's just be acquaintances. I can never be your friend again. I'm happy to help you with the sale of your songs. But Jesse, do not sell them cheaply. You have a great talent and you need to get a fair price for your music."

"I need you to be my business manager if nothing else," Jesse said.

She shook her head. "What you need and what I need are two different things." Cass walked away and went below deck to her room. She pulled the trunk in front of the door, took a joint from her pocket and lit up. She lay on her bunk and smoked. Jesse would never learn. He couldn't have everything he wanted. It was hard for him to realize that Cass didn't want him in her life anymore.

However, she was tempted by Tony. They had always gotten along, but not a whole lot of excitement between them. Maybe she would get in touch with him again when she returned to L.A. Yes, she definitely would. She liked singing with the band again, although she knew her heart was not into surfing songs, but more into the creative, poetic words that Jesse crafted. She instinctively knew that San Francisco music was the path to the future.

⤸

The next morning Cass was getting dressed when someone knocked at her door. She threw on a housecoat and opened the door. It was Tony. He had a back-pack on his shoulders and a satchel in his hand.

"Morning. I'm about to shove off and I wanted to connect with you again." He stepped forward and suddenly embraced Cass. He leaned down and kissed her on the lips.

"I just want you to remember what we had and remind you to call me when you return to L.A."

Cass was a little breathless but smiled and stepped out of his arms. "I will call, Tony. And I do remember what we had."

He stepped back into the hall and went up top. Jesse was standing at the top of the stairs and only saw Tony come out of Cass's room. He stepped aside as Tony and then Cass came up on deck.

"So long everyone. Thanks Howard for the hospitality." He waved to Howard and the group on deck and went down the gangplank. The rest of the band was already in the van. Tony slid into the driver's seat and drove away from the Van Damme.

Jesse walked over to Cass. His anger was apparent. "Did he spend the night with you?"

Cass looked at him. "I don't believe you. It's not your business, Jesse. Leave it and me alone." She moved away to sit with Howard and Lia at the table.

Jesse grabbed her arm. "Answer me."

Cass stopped. Howard jumped up and gently unwound Jesse's hand from Cass's arm.

"Jesse, you don't want to be doing this," Howard said.

Jesse dropped his arm. "I'm sorry, Cass. I shouldn't have done that."

Cass moved away and sat next to Lia. "Listen to me, Jesse," Cass said. "Don't ever touch me again like that or I'll punch you in the nose."

For some reason this tickled Jesse and he laughed. "I'll bet you would, too."

He pulled a roll of bills from his pocket and laid them in front of Howard. "$2500. Thanks for bailing me out. I have to go write some more songs now so I can pay Bartok back."

Jesse went down the gangplank and headed for his boat.

30

John and Claire had been seeing each other for several weeks and they hoped Jesse was still in the dark about their relationship.

They were sitting on Claire's bunk practicing Jesse's latest creation. "You know, John. We need to tell Jesse about us so we don't have to sneak around anymore. I'm an adult and I can do what I want with my life."

"I was thinking the same thing. He'll probably be freaked. He's so unpredictable," John replied.

"The sooner we do it the better. Let's go to his boat this morning and tell him before practice, before the others get there."

After John and Claire had coffee and toast on deck, he helped her get down the gangplank with her walker and they headed for Jesse's boat.

Kayak greeted them on deck. He had been sunning himself. John called into the cabin. "Jesse. Can you come up?"

Jesse appeared in his swimming trunks and a tee-shirt. "Hi. What's up?"

"We have something to tell you," Claire said. "John and I are in a relationship. We care about each other and we're tired of sneaking around so you wouldn't find out."

Jesse looked at both of them and smiled. "I know... what else is new?"

"You mean you knew and you never said anything?" Claire said.

"I figured you'd tell me when you were ready." He looked at John. "Take care of my baby sister. If you hurt her I'll break your arm." He smiled and hit him gently on the shoulder.

John smiled in relief. "Hey brother, are we practicing today?"

"Yup. The other guys will be here around one. Claire, you learned the words to that song yet?"

Claire nodded. "I have. Cass helped me for a couple of days. I got it."

"I want you to sing louder. Practice that. Okay?"

She nodded.

"We'll be back around one," John said. He and Claire walked off the boat. He helped her onto the dock. She was becoming more agile with her walker.

⌇

Lia and Howard sat on deck of the Van Damme feeding the sea gulls pieces of old bread. The sun was shining hot on the wood railing. Lia threw a piece of bread in the air as an acrobatic gull grabbed it.

"Howard, I've decided to stay up here. I went to Berkeley UC the other day and transferred my files. I will register next month for classes. I'll finish my senior year and go ahead and get my doctorate. " She turned toward him.

Howard embraced her. "Wonderful, babe. I'm so

happy you decided to do this. What changed your mind?"

"You and our relationship and the kids; all of those things."

"I'll get us an apartment in Berkeley when my lease is up here in September. I'll find a job in Berkeley. My friend works at a book store on Telegraph, Cody's. I'll try there first."

Lia held her hand out and a gull snatched the bread from her fingers. "I have to drive down to L.A. and pick up my things and give notice to my apartment manager."

"Okay. I wish I could go with you but I need to be here for the last month of gigs at The Ark."

"I know. Cass is going to go with me. She has decided to return to L.A."

"Think she and Jesse are finished?"

"I think so. Cass is not about to put up with Jesse as an old man. He can't be a one woman man and that's what she wants."

"I feel badly for Jesse that he's throwing away a good woman." Howard broke up another piece of bread.

"He is, but he doesn't know it. Cass will get over it. She has plenty of gigs to look forward to in L.A. She'll get back with her friends that she played and sang with." Lia changed the subject. "Did you know that Claire and John have a relationship going?"

Howard looked surprised. "No shit? I hadn't noticed. Good for them. They seem like a good pair."

Lia's thought flew back to herself and Howard. "I'll leave a week before classes start at UC and have time to clear out my life in L.A."

"We need to start looking for an apartment before they're all taken. The kids come back early looking for housing."

"Okay with me. The sooner the better. I was wondering if I could drive your van down to L.A. and leave my MG with you? I would like to rent a trailer and bring back some of my furniture."

"Sure babe, but you need me to help. Maybe I'll fly down to L.A. the day before and we can drive back together."

"Sounds like a plan," Lisa said smiling. She felt like her life was coming together with Howard.

"What about the kids?"

"I'll see if Bartok will take care of them for a couple of days. Let's go over to Berkeley today and look for apartments."

"Okay. I'll get the kids ready." Lia threw her last piece of bread to the winds and several gulls fought over it.

↩

Cass picked up her guitar and walked on stage to start her set. The place was still not crowded so she tuned up slowly. She decided to play Jesse's song, *Together Again*. It had a haunting melody in a minor key and her voice sounded great singing it. Strumming the opening chords, she sang the first verse;

"Love comes but once a lifetime.
If we miss the signs,
Like a fork without tines,
We starve for the food we need."

Cass's voice was strong and clear tonight. She saw David, Spence and John come into the coffee house and walked on stage to play back-up for her. They picked up right where she was in the song. She continued to sing Jesse's lovely song. Her eyes were closed and she had a smile on her lips. When she looked up she saw Jesse standing in the doorway with his guitar slung over his shoulder. He walked to the stage and motioned to her if he could come up. She nodded. He positioned himself just behind her to her right and they continued the song. Jesse took over the melody and Cass began singing the harmony. All of the musicians did a bang up job of performing, *Together Again*. When they were finished the audience applauded loudly. Cass thanked them over the mike and then started singing one of her songs, *Pretty Polly*. The guys continued to accompany her and Jesse sang harmony to her melody on the chorus. After *Pretty Polly*, Cass sang three or four of her songs in her repertoire, then left the stage. David, Spence, John and Jesse left too, as another performer got ready to do a set.

Cass returned her guitar to its case and Jesse came over.

"That was a lovely set, Cass. I wish you'd reconsider and play with the band again. We sounded fab out there. You aced it, babe."

"Don't think so, Jesse. You have Claire. She is a good strong lead singer."

"She don't sing loud enough. We can't hear her over the electric guitars."

"You'll just have to work with her on that. She's a very good singer."

Jesse came up close to Cass and put his hand on her arm. "I want you back in the band, Cass. You have a charisma on stage that's hard to find."

She looked straight into his beautiful eyes. "Jesse, I made my decision. You have to abide by it. I'm not interested in singing with you and the band, anymore. I'm splitting and going to L.A. with Lia in a couple of weeks to resume my life there."

Jesse looked stricken; His face drained of color and he began to perspire. "Oh no, babe. Don't do that. I'm sorry I'm not a good old man, but you are a basic part of the Desperados. We need you."

"Sorry, Jesse."

"Cass, I care about you a lot. Please always remember that. I'm sorry we couldn't make a go of it." He squeezed her arm gently.

"I'm sorry too, Jesse." She put her hand over Jesse's.

He picked up her hand and kissed her fingers."Catch you later."

She picked up her guitar and walked away. Heading below deck to her room she stashed her guitar and sat on her bed wondering about the conversation she'd just had with Jesse. He really seemed to want her in the band, but of course she wasn't going to do it. She had resigned herself to returning to L.A. and staying away from him. Not knowing what he was doing or with whom helped her get over him. There was no going back to him or the band. She didn't need them and she was pretty sure they didn't need her either. Claire was a great substitute for a lead singer. She would grow into the role. Cass would help her with the songs before she left.

Cass went back up to the coffee house and sat at a table listening to the music and performers. David, Spence and John motioned her over to their table. Claire had joined them. She went reluctantly.

"That was cool, Cass. We still got the magic together," John whispered.

"Thanks," Cass whispered back.

Claire grabbed her hand. "Cass will you help me with Jesse's new song tomorrow?"

Cass nodded. They all sat back to listen to the trio on stage singing Peter, Paul and Mary songs.

31

Jesse lit the bong and handed it to Emily the groupie he had invited to spend the night on his boat. She took a large hit and handed it back. They smoked until the hash was gone. They drank a bottle of Thunderbird wine, did up some Heroin and Jesse was feeling no pain. Emily was curled up on the bed with eyes closed. Kayak was asleep in a corner.

The storm had rolled in around five o'clock in the late afternoon, bringing a rain front and rocking all the boats at Gate Six like a Beach Boys performance. The wind was so fierce that the bong slid around on Jesse's table.

He woke up around midnight and decided to check the anchor. Staggering up the steps to the deck he realized he'd forgotten to tie down the bow line to the dock. But first, he leaned over the side to check the anchor. He felt instant vertigo, losing his balance and falling overboard head first and straight down into the murky Bay of Sausalito. The first rush of cold water caused him to inhale automatically, taking a deep gasp of water into his lungs. Putting his arms out he tried to stop his descent, but it didn't work. Spiraling downward he felt the depth of the dark underwater world. Thoughts of Cass came immediately into his mind. Then he thought of his music; no longer able to sing and play. No more Cass, no more sail boat, no more Kayak. All the things he held dear were gone in the gasp of a breath. Why couldn't he have made it work with Cass? He knew he was drowning. Panic set in and he took a huge gulp of water automatically, not thinking. Choking and sputtering and gagging was one of the last physical feelings Jesse experienced. As his lungs shut down, his mind still wandered. Would anyone ever hear his music?

Back in the cabin of Jesse's sailboat, Kayak was awake and whining at the door.

⌐

The storm had rocked the Van Damme all night long in spite of its being in dry-dock. Enough water splashed upon the hull to make the boat pitch and undulate like a small earthquake.

Cass awoke with a start. She had slept fitfully, having bad dreams. Sounds of shouting and crying came from above. She put on her robe, brushed her hair briefly and headed up on deck. She saw Lia and Howard, and Claire sobbing on John's shoulder, David, Spence and Bartok, and a groupie standing with two policemen, in a cluster. Bartok and Howard had tears on their cheeks.

She rushed over to Lia. "What happened?"

Lia turned to Cass and put her arm around her shoulders. "Jesse is dead. He drowned last night. Probably fell off his boat. His body was found this morning early by a fisherman at the end of Waldo Point."

Cass felt like she was in quicksand. She couldn't move her arms, hands or mouth. She was having a terrible dream. The nightmare she'd had last night.

Finally she found her voice. "No," she cried out.

Cass's face was as white as a fresh snow fall. Two red spots formed in the center of her cheeks. She inhaled deeply having trouble catching her breath.

The two policemen came over to where Claire, John, Lia, Howard and Cass were standing.

"I'll need someone to identify the body. You the sister?" one of the policemen asked Claire.

Claire was incoherent still sobbing on John's shoulder. "I can identify him," John offered.

"She's in no shape to do it."

John introduced himself and the rest of the group. The policeman took their names. "The coroner will be here shortly," the blue coat said. "The body will go down to the morgue. If you can come down today we'd appreciate it."

"Can I see him now?" Cass asked.

The policeman nodded. "He's down at the end of the dock."

Cass rushed below deck and hurriedly struggled into her jeans and tee shirt. Back on deck, while Bartok comforted Claire, Lia and Howard dutifully followed Cass down the gangplank of the Van Damme and walked with her to the end of the dock.

Jesse's body was laid out on the planks. His face was gray, and his hair had seaweed intertwined with his curls making him look like a sea urchin. Blue shorts were bunched around his crotch. Hands were closed, as were his eyes.

Cass kneeled down beside him and stroked his brow. "Jesse, why were you so reckless?" she whispered to him. She kissed his cheek and stood. Lia and Howard took her arms and turned her around back to the Van Damme.

Finally the tears came. She sobbed all the way back to the ferry boat. Lia and Howard had their arms around her. The groupie, Emily was leaving the boat just as Cass, Lia and Howard went up the gangplank.

"I didn't know he had fallen overboard. He was gone all night and I didn't' know where he was." She was crying too.

"It wasn't your fault," Cass said kindly.

Emily got into a police car and was driven away.

"Apparently she is a runaway form Oregon. The police will return her to her parents," Bartok said.

John, Claire, David and Spence, Howard and Bartok were sitting around the picnic table on deck. Claire's eyes were swollen and red.

"Cass, come join us. We have a proposition," John said. Kayak was lying at John's feet.

Cass, Lia and Howard sat on chairs. John cleared his throat. "We've decided to play the remaining gigs this month at the Drinking Gourd in SF and give our proceeds to Bartok to help pay him back for the bail money he put up for Jesse."

He paused. "Would you consider singing with the band for the next four weeks? We think Jesse would want us to do this."

Cass dried her tears. "You have Claire as lead singer."

"True," John continued, "but we could use your strong voice and it would help Claire out too. We have a contract and we hate to break it. It would hurt our reputation as a band."

Cass thought about the suggestion. She wasn't in any big hurry to get back to L.A. She cared about the guys and Claire and the band's future and she made an instant decision. "I will do it if Lia will wait to drive back to L.A. until we finish the gig at the Gourd," Cass said.

Lia nodded. "No problem."

John got up and hugged Cass. "Thanks, girl. You're outta' sight."

The following Friday, four days after Jesse's death, the Desperados were playing their gig at the Drinking Gourd.

They were all on stage, tuning up when John took the mike. "We all want you to know our founder and creative genius behind this band, Jesse Powers died on Monday night of this week."

An audible moan went through the audience.

"We want to dedicate this month's gig here at the Drinking Gourd to Jesse. Here's Jesse's latest creation, *Jesse's Song*."

John and David broke out into an upbeat tempo, Spence on drums and Claire and Cass singing lead.

The song was autobiographical, about Jesse's search for his way in this life. The harmony was in a minor key and mournful. Cass almost cried during a couple of verses. Claire did have tears running down her face. She choked up at one point and Cass carried the melody.

The band communicated completely with each other for the next two hours, playing one of their best performances. Cass actually enjoyed herself in spite of the bittersweet event. Claire finally moved into the musical mood and carried her part.

Several beers were sent up to the stage for the musicians. The guys sipped theirs' but Cass and Claire did not drink.

After the gig, everyone was packing up when Mike, the manager walked over to the band. "Hey, thanks for continuing the gig. We didn't have a backup to fill in. We're damn sorry about Jesse. He was a talented musician."

"Thanks for letting us continue without Jesse," John said.

"I think people will come here to hear the band when the news gets out," Mike said.

And sure enough, The Drinking Gourd was packed for the remainder of the month of August.

⌐

No one knew where Jesse's parents were performing with the circus. Claire sometimes got a postcard from them, but she hadn't heard from them recently. Until she did, they couldn't notify them of Jesse's death.

The Sausalito police department dropped the charges against Jesse as he was deceased. Cass and Bartok paid for a burial site in the little cemetery on the hill above the city. All of Jesse's friends, the Boat Community and his sister and Cass were at the gravesite. Cass had looked for a passage that could be read at Jesse's graveside. She came up with something from Shakespeare. John read:

"Not marble, nor gilded monuments of princes
Shall out live this powerful rhyme;
But you shall shine more bright in these contents
Than unswept stone
Besmeared with sluttish time."

Claire threw a rose as did Cass on the casket and John threw a handful of dirt into the grave. John picked up his guitar and he and David played a parting tune, one of Jesse's, *Together Again*. Cass and Claire sang in pure sweet voices which flowed across the cemetery like a dirge.

Once they were back on the Van Damme Lia and Cass prepared a meal for everyone and they toasted and smoked Jesse way into the night.

↩

Howard's VW van raced across the Golden Gate Bridge, windows open, the cool breeze blowing Lia's and Cass's long manes into the wind. The sun was especially warm and the gulls were out in force.

Lia stole a glance at Cass. "Are you sad to leave Sausalito?"

"On one level, yes. I made some cool friends while I was there this summer. But I'm eager to get back to my L.A. life."

"You'll have to come up to see Howard and me occasionally. We'll be living in Berkeley."

"Oh course, I will. Keep me posted on how the band is doing, and on Claire and John."

"I think they are talking marriage, although God knows why they want to do that.

Marriage is kind of out-moded these days, but I think John wants to protect Claire as much as he can. If he's her husband, he has more leverage."

"Yeah, I can dig that," Cass said. "They seemed to be happy living on Jesse's boat with Kayak and playing gigs around the Bay Area."

"I think John wants to protect her from her parents as well and support her through her grief." Lia merged into the 19th Street traffic on their way south.

"That makes sense. But Claire is pretty independent these days. She gets around real well with her cane."

"How you handling Jesse's death?" Lia glanced at Cass.

"I miss him and I'm still grieving for him, but life will go on for me. I already disconnected from him emotionally, but I never dreamed he would be gone from the music scene here. I just can't help feeling so sad that the world has lost a great talent. He could have been a great song writer, Lia. And I'm sad that we couldn't work things out between us. I think I did love him. I just couldn't deal with infidelity again."

"I understand. I hope the band can continue to play his music so he isn't forgotten," Lia said. "John mentioned they had a lot of gigs lined up with Jesse's death in the news."

"It's a shame that it takes a tragedy like this to get an artist's music out to the public."

"Yep. What do you intend doing once you get settled again in L.A.?"

Cass thought a minute. "I want to get back in touch with the old group and see if there's room for me again in their group. I might try to get back on the newspaper again." She thought she'd get in touch with Tony, too. Memories of their times together came surging back.

Lia nodded. "Hey babe, did you have any epiphanies or profound realizations this summer?"

Cass contemplated that thought. "I did. I realized with Faye committing suicide and Jesse's recklessness that life is what you make it. Claire has shown incredible courage and strength to be able to walk with just a cane. You can be happy or distressed, anything you want to arrange for yourself. It's all up to each of us. Bartok taught me that. He's so content with his life. You and Howard have made a niche for the two of you and the kids. I admire that in both of you."

Cass knew she wanted to continue her life in the music scene but she also knew it was very unstable. Being a reporter was a steady job and brought in the same pay every week. If she had learned anything from Jesse it was, not to take second best. She knew what she wanted in a relationship and she would hold out for just that. Love, well that might have to take a back burner for her right now. She had been burned by Jesse and she wasn't hankering to get hurt again anytime soon.

Lia smiled. "Thanks. I never thought when I came up here that Howard and I would last, but we have, so far. I guess what I've learned is to take one day at a time. Be grateful for small gifts. Make love a major part of my existence. Life is good today. Tomorrow I'll wake up with that thought in mind."

Cass squeezed Lia's arm. "Take one day at a time and be grateful for small gifts. Right on!"

To order additional copies of this
book: www.colleenraenovels.com
or www.createspace.com/6250573

Made in the USA
Las Vegas, NV
12 October 2021